The Hands Resist Him is a painting created by artist William Stoneham in 1972. The macabre painting was listed for sale on the internet auction site eBay in 2000. The listing stated that the painting was cursed, and claimed that the boy and doll represented in the painting would come out of the painting at night.

This haunting is what compelled the sellers to list it. They did so with a warning and a disclaimer that absolved them from any supernatural events that might occur to or around anyone who becomes in possession of it.

The painting quickly secured a World wide infamy. It is the World's first Internet paranormal legend, and has become a Global viral internet meme. It has been the subject of multiple magazine articles and was part of a BBC documentary. It continues to captivate an audience World Wide.

I would like to thank William Stoneham for his support of this book and to acknowledge his incredible artistic talent.

Darren Kyle O'Neill

Artist: William Stoneham

'The Hands Resist Him' © Darren Kyle O'Neill

home | my eBay | site map | sign in

HAUNTED PAINTING —— WARNING AND DISCLAIMER
Item #251789217
Antiques & Art:Art:Fine:Paintings

	Currently	$1,025.00	First bid	$199.00
	Quantity	1	# of bids	30 (bid history) (with emails)
			Location	EAST LOS ANGELES VAULT
			Country	United States
	Started	Feb-01-00 07:32:28 PST	(☑ mail this auction to a friend)	
	Ends	Feb-11-00 07:32:28 PST	(☐ request a gift alert)	
			Featured & Featured Category Auction	
(to seller) (to bidder)	Seller (Rating)	mrnoreserve (51) ☆		
		(view comments in seller's Feedback Profile) (view seller's other auctions) (ask seller a question)		
If you are the seller or the high bidder - now what?	High bid	ionia7 (11) ☆		
	Payment	Money Order/Cashiers Checks, Personal Checks		
	Shipping	Buyer pays actual shipping charges, Seller ships internationally (worldwide)		
	Relist item	Seller: Didn't sell your item the first time? eBay will refund your relisting fee if it sells the second time around. Relist this item.		

Seller assumes all responsibility for listing this item. You should contact the seller to resolve any questions before bidding. Auction currency is U.S. dollars ($) unless otherwise noted.

Description

WHEN WE RECEIVED THIS PAINTING, WE THOUGHT IT WAS REALLY GOOD ART. A "PICKER " HAD FOUND IT ABANDONNED BEHIND AN OLD BREWERY. AT HTE TIME WE WONDERED A LITLLE WHY A SEEMINGLY PERFECTLY FINE PAINTING WOULD BE DISCARDED LIKE THAT. (TODAY WE DON'T !!!) ONE MORNING OUR 4 AND 1/2 YEAR OLD DAUGHTER CLAIMED, THAT THE CHILDREN IN THE PICTURE WERE FIGHTING, AND COMING INTO THE ROOM DURING THE NIGHT. NOW, I DON'T BELIEVE IN UFOS OR ELVIS BEING ALIVE, BUT MY HUSBAND WAS ALARMED TO MY AMUSEMENT HE SET UP A MOTION TRIGGERED CAMREA FOR THE NIGHTS. AFTER THREE NIGHTS THERE WERE PICTURES. THE LAST TWO PICTURES SHOWN ARE FROM THAT STAKEOUT. AFTER SEEING THE BOY SEEMINGLY EXITING THE PAINTING UNDER THREAT, WE DECIDED, THE PAINTING HAS TO GO. PLEASE JUDGE FOR YOURSELF. --- BEFORE YOU DO, PLEASE READ THE FOLLOWIND WARNING AND DISCLAIMER. ----WARNING: DO NOT BID ON THIS PAINTING IF YOU ARE SUCCEPTIBLE TO STRESS RELATED DISEASE, FAINT OF HEART OR ARE UNFAMILIAR WITH SUPERNATURAL EVENTS. BY BIDDING ON THIS PAINTING, YOU AGREE TO RELEASE THE OWNERS OF ALL LIABILITY IN RELATION TO THE SALE OR ANY EVENTS HAPPENING AFTER THE SALE, THAT MIGHT BE CONTRIBUTED TO THIS PAINTING. THIS PAINTING MAY OR MAY NOT POSSESS SUPERNATURAL POWERS, THAT COULD IMPACT OR CHANGE YOUR LIFE. HOWEVER, BY BIDDING YOU AGREE TO EXCLUSIVELY BID ON THE VALUE OF THE ARTWORK, WITH DISREGARD TO THE LAST TWO PHOTOS FEATURED IN THIS AUCTION, AND HOLD THE OWNERS HARMLESS IN REGARD TO THEM AND THEIR IMPACT, EXPRESSED OR IMPLIED.------------- NOW THAT WE GOT THIS OUT OF THE WAY, ONE QUESTION TO YOU EBAYERS. WE WANT OUR HOUSE TO BE BLESSED AFTER THE PAINTING IS GONE, DOES ANYBODY KNOW, WHO IS QUALIFIED TO DO THAT?

On Feb-02-00 at 11:36:21 PST, seller added the following information:

THE SIZE OF THE PAINTING IS 24 BY 36 INCHES, SO IT IS RATHER LARGE. AS I HAVE HAD SEVERAL QUESTIONS, HERE THE FOLLOWING ANSWERS. THERE WAS NO ODOR LEFT BEHIND IN THE ROOM. THERE WERE NO VOICES, OR THE SMELL OF GUNPOWDER, NO FOODPRINTS OR STRANGE FLUIDS ON THE WALL. TO DETER QUESTIONS IN THIS DIRECTION, THERE ARE NO GHOSTS IN THIS WORLD, NO SUPERNATURAL POWERS, THIS IS JUST A PAINTING, AND MOST THESE THINGS HAVE AN EXPLANATION, IN THIS CASE PROBABLY A FLUKE LIGHT EFFECT. I ENCOURAGE YOU TO BID ON THE ARTWORK, AND CONSIDER THE LAST TWO PHOTOGRAPHS AS PURE ENTERTAINMENT, AND PLEASE DO NOT TAKE THEM INTO CONSIDERATION, WHEN BIDDING. AS WE THINK IT IS A GOOD IDEA TO BLESS ANY HOUSE, WE STILL WELCOME INPUT INTO THAT PROCEDURE.

On Feb-11-00 at 21:05:57 PST, seller added the following information:

This auction is nearing the end. I want to thank the more than 13000 people that took the time to look at this image on ebay. I appreciate the more than 30 suggestions, that I received regarding blessing the house, exorcising and cleansing. 7 emails reported strange or irregular events taking place, when viewing this image. And I will relay two suggestions made by the senders. First not to use this image as the background on the screen, and second not to display this image around juveniles or children. Last not least, thanks for apreciating the art as well.

Be Careful What You Bid For

12 February 2000

narcissus77 hit the refresh button with her black fingernail.

You're the highest bidder.

She refreshed again. The refresh sent the page dark for a fleeting moment, but enough time for narcissus77 to see her reflection on the screen. She didn't like it, not at all. In fact, it gave her a sharp chill. But infuriatingly she couldn't deny its honesty. It's not like looking at yourself in a mirror, when you're subconsciously prepared, you pull *that face*; but it's when you don't expect to see yourself, that's when you really see yourself. Her ego had been assaulted, I mean she knows who she is, she's Ms. Hawaiian Tropic 1995. That was five years ago when she was just eighteen, beautiful with blonde hair, a tan and copper eye makeup. Now she's beautiful with black hair, no tan and black makeup, and she knows very well that the '95 contest was the toughest line-up of any year to date; that's what everyone said.

She allowed herself to be happy in her position of highest bidder.

izzy1969 was made of sharper stuff.

"Stupid moron, you're just bringing the price up by bidding early. I'll wait, then I'll strike at around seven seconds, and you'll be all 'what the? who the?' and like that. Beard! What's with you?"

izzy1969 waited for a response. People do that, they ask their pet something and then wait for response. Beard, a brute of a Rottweiler, wanted to respond. If he'd been able to, his response probably would have been: Why are you staring at a glowing box, or, Where's my dinner? Instead, he gave a diplomatic woof-growl, but he kept it a low-key hesitant response; he didn't want to get into trouble, you understand, by saying the wrong thing.

*

The face behind eBayer 'Leydenx4' was Daniel Leyden,

orthodontist, husband and father, who scored highly on all three. He

leaned forward on a smoked glass coffee table, moved aside two

empty champagne glasses and opened up his laptop. He did so with

suspect coordination. His wife had given in to her coordination

problem by lying on the sofa behind him.

"What are you doing?" she asked with a hint of a slur,

especially on the word "doing," which kind of faded halfway. Daniel

turned and looked down at her around the small of his back. He had

a glazed look about the eyes.

"I'm gonna buy something on eBay for us, an anim-versary

present."

Patricia laughed. "Wow, you're cooked, huh, an anniversary

present," she stressed the correct pronunciation. Daniel smiled,

pointed at her and winked.

Patricia collected herself enough to pull together some

authority in her voice and sat up to the right of Daniel, squinting at

his laptop screen.

"No, Daniel, they say you should never buy something on

eBay when you're drunk." Daniel picked up an empty glass. He tried to drink from it, and then he looked at it, bewildered as to why no liquid went into his mouth. He realized it was because it was empty. He reached for the bottle and tried to aim it over his wife's glass, but he struggled; as if it was two opposing magnets, he just couldn't get it centered. When it was almost over the mouth of one of the flutes, he went for the pour, but the bottle was empty.

"All that for a dead soldier," he mumbled dejectedly as he placed the bottle back on the coffee table, hitting the glass top too hard. "Anyway," he cried energetically, "*they*, the famous and elusive *they*, they, also say you *must* buy something on eBay when you're drunk at least once in your life."

Patricia raised an eyebrow. She continued to watch his screen, her chin balanced on her hand, her elbow balanced on her knee.

They were interrupted by a knock on the door.

"Come in," said Daniel.

Jessica, the Leydens' sixteen-year-old babysitter, tentatively popped her head around the door clutching her babysitting money. "They're asleep, I went into their room, and they're asleep, can I go now?"

"Sure, thanks Jessica, is your mom there?" responded Patricia. Jessica walked out into the hall and opened the front door. Across the street was her mother, waiting at their door. Jessica waved, her mother waved back and pointed to her watch. Jessica shouted back into the living room. "Yes, Mrs. Leyden, she's right there with the door open."

"Hold on," said Daniel. "Come back here for a sec?"

Jessica walked back into the living room.

Daniel continued, "Let me see your teeth."

Jessica smiled, showing her braces. "I'm keeping the braces clean, Dr. Leyden, don't worry."

Daniel smiled. "I know, Jessica, a few more weeks and I'll take them off."

Jessica giggled excitedly. "I know, I can't wait! Good night." Jessica left the house and gently closed the front door.

"She's such a nice kid. Now, where were we?" said Daniel. He clicked "Ending soonest" and a jumble of items filled the page. Each time Daniel saw something he liked, Patricia nudged him with her left knee and so he moved on, that took care of the speedboat, the

Harley-Davidson and the telescope. Scrolling through, Daniel paused on an item, a painting with a tiny dark thumbnail.

Patricia said inquisitively, *"The Hands Resist Him."* She paused. "Click on it."

Daniel clicked on the image, a full window opened of the image. It was of a boy standing outside a shop, beside him stood a doll holding a dry battery cell. Behind them, through a glass door, armless hands could be dimly seen reaching toward the boy. Daniel scrolled down and began to read the text accompanying the listing out loud.

"When we received this painting, we thought it was really good art. The person we bought it from found it abandoned in an old brewery. At the time, we wondered why a seemingly perfectly fine painting would be discarded like that. Today we don't. One morning our four-and-a-half-year old daughter claimed that the children in the picture were fighting, and coming into the room during the night. Now, I don't believe in UFOs or Elvis being alive, but my husband was alarmed. To my amusement, he set up a motion-triggered camera for three nights. After three nights, there were pictures. The last two pictures shown are from that stakeout. After seeing the boy seemingly exit the painting as if under threat, we decided the painting has to go. Please judge for yourself. Before you do, please read the following warning and disclaimer."

Patricia read: "Warning! Do not bid on this painting if you are susceptible to stress-related diseases, faint of heart or are unfamiliar with supernatural events. By bidding on this painting, you agree to release the owners of all liability in relation to the sale or any events happening after the sale that might be attributed to this painting. This painting may or may not possess supernatural powers that could impact or change your life. However, by bidding you agree to bid exclusively on the value of the artwork, disregarding to the last two photos featured in this auction. You agree not to hold the previous owners responsible for any untoward events that may occur after purchase."

Patricia tried to make light of it, as did Daniel. They both smiled, but their smiles betrayed them, they were both suddenly quite sober. "Well, you're not thinking of bidding, are you?" asked Patricia.

"Why not?" said an excited Daniel. "You don't believe in this crap, do you?"

Patricia wasn't really sure what crap she might or might not believe in, and neither was Daniel. She responded with an alternative argument, "But it's such a weird anniversary present." Daniel didn't respond, he just stared at the screen, as did Patricia. They both studied the item intensely. Patricia said softly, "Just don't put it in the kids' room."

Daniel scrolled up to the listing information. It listed narcissus77 as highest bidder, with six minutes left. "Six minutes," said a determined Daniel. "I know how this works, I'll be patient."

*

Mambo66, on the other hand, was impatient. He hated being outbid, besides a night security guard hasn't got much else to do. You can't even look out the windows, only at the windows. You're forced to see your own lonely life in all its reflected misery, and the reflected misery of all of your lonely life props, your monitor, your security uniform that doesn't suit you, the big ugly board behind you that lists the names and floors of the corporate monsters housed within the building.

Mambo66 stood up and with his best New York accent on max, torpedoed, "So you think I can't afford three hundred bucks, huh? Take that, yah basta-ad!" He hit the "Return" key with his downturned thumb, maximizing the moment with a bid and an insult. He sat down again.

You're the highest bidder.

"You're damn right."

He slouched back in the chair with an air of satisfaction, his hands clasped behind his head. Such nice moments (however small), are to be savored, and indeed he savored this. Or he tried to, but a little voice inside him knew just how small this victory was. In fact, the little voice reminded him it wasn't even a victory at all, as the bidding was still not over. This little shit of a voice wanted to snatch this fragile moment from Mambo66. Give the man a bone, for Christ's sake.

Mambo66 stared at his reflection, but not at himself, "Hey ... fuck you," and bang! It worked, the little shit of a voice's last comment was vaporized out of existence and the memory of it deleted. With the little shit of a voice defeated, he could go back to his moment undisturbed. However, the moment was still about to prematurely snatched from him. Not by anything, not by the little shit of a voice, a shrill phone call, or a car horn, but by nothing. Suddenly, nothing was upon him, louder than a shrill phone call or a car horn, and yet, from this nothing, from this non-thing, this non-entity, there was indeed something, something that terrified Mambo66. It enveloped him so totally and utterly that it rendered him almost incapacitated. He couldn't identify what it was, but he knew something was about to happen, something bad, very bad. He had no idea what, or even how something can even be born from nothing, but he knew. He felt a sick certainty in his stomach, just as certainly as if his feet were nailed to a diabolical conveyer belt taking him to a place he mustn't go, a place that he must not, under any circumstances, be taken. He would gladly kill himself first.

"Holy shit, what?" His chest felt very heavy, he struggled to expand his lungs. His pulse felt like it was counting down, like a timer on a bomb.

"Is someone there?" He paused, said it again, but this time he screamed it, revealing to himself the disturbing sound of the terror in his voice. "Is someone there?"

Ex-marine Mambo66 once killed an enemy sniper whom he had tracked to the sniper's family home. He did it up close with a shovel thrown to him by the sniper's wife, the wife the sniper enjoyed regularly beating. She did not hesitate, and neither did Mambo66. Yet this same Mambo66 was in terror, a terror much worse than anything he had ever experienced in a combat situation.

"Oh God, someone, please help," he pleaded to a cruel savior who would never come. He stepped backwards, pressing his back against the ugly corporate board, even now, the ugly board made no attempt to offer any more friendship than it normally did.

The lights went out, not blink-blink then out, but clonk and out.

Mambo66 fumbled for his flashlight in his desk drawer, he pleaded again to that absent savior with all of his lungs, "Help me!" He momentarily felt the cold steel flashlight in among whatever else he had forgotten was in there, but he had released it before realizing it was the flashlight, so he continued searching. A sharp pin of some sort stuck in his finger, right between the finger and nail.

He found the flashlight, and this time he held onto it like the hand of a lifeguard.

Only now that he had it did he realize how useless it was. It had a bright beam, but a narrow beam with crisp sharp edges from anything in view to complete blackness. He ran to the direction of the front door, it was locked shut, attached to the same fuse that had put out the lights. He needed to get to get to the fuses. He stumbled along the corridor, feeling his way with his left hand, the small circle of light created from the flashlight shone like the light seen from the bottom of a well. How he wished he was up in the light, but he was in the darkness at the bottom of the well. Something rushed past the tiny beam, and he stopped. He quickly whipped the flashlight from side to side in a frenzied panic. Again, he caught a glimpse of something, but it was again gone, in the blackness, on the wrong side of the light. He knew he was not alone in this dark well. He turned, pointing the flashlight at the black windows, the bright light outlining his reflected silhouette.

Standing behind him to his right was another silhouette, a small silhouette. Quickly and accurately he spun around. The nothing that was terrorizing him was now in view; a small boy with his back to him, crew cut blond hair, a light blue T-shirt and shorts cut just above the knee, shoes and socks. This wasn't a child from the second millennium. To Mambo66, there was no doubt that this wasn't a child at all.

The silence was pierced, a flat, resonating cry. The sound filled everything and inflicted everything, every space outside or inside the mind was violated. The boy began to turn, but he was turning very, very slowly, so slowly, in fact, that maybe he wasn't turning at all. Maybe it just seemed like he was turning. Mambo66 tried to stifle a scream, not because he was ashamed to scream, but because he was too scared to scream. Instead he just managed to gulp air and make strange gargling noises.

The lights came back on, and the boy was gone. Mambo66 dropped his flashlight and crumpled to the floor. He began to cry in a way that he hadn't since the day before his twenty-seventh birthday. The cries came from a place with which he was unfamiliar, and had a sound with which he was unfamiliar. They were loud, agonizing and so very sad. A stranger walked past the building's thick double-glazed enormous floor-to-ceiling windows and saw this silent spectacle of despair. She didn't stop and question why, she pulled up her collar as they made eye contact. *Whatever's this man's problem, it's his; thank God it's not mine.*

He dragged himself up and made his way back to his desk, but he made sure he opened the building's front door first, and put a heavy chrome cylinder trash can next to it, just in case.

He looked at his screen.

You have been outbid.

He pulled the pin from his nail, a reminder that he didn't dream it all.

*

Beard was busy eating.

izzy1969 was animated. He was staring at his laptop. He turned to Beard, "OK, so I couldn't resist. I know, I know, four minutes left, but sometimes I forget, so this way at least I've got a bid in."

Beard suddenly broke away from his food and scrambled backwards in panic, his paws slipping on the marble floor. He snarled and barked ferociously all around him as if chasing invisible wasps.

izzy1969 bolted up out of his chair. "What the hell? What happened? What's wrong?" izzy1969 was taken aback at this display.

Beard stopped. He fixed his gaze on the bathroom door and began to growl deeply, slowly revealing his eager and very capable teeth. Then he then began to bark with intensity and real purpose.

izzy1969 was scared, he had never seen such aggression in his dog. "Boy, what is it? You ain't kidding, are you? The bathroom? Go take a look."

izzy1969 walked behind Beard and tried to persuade him to go to the bathroom with a gentle nudge of his slippered foot. But Beard, as angry and ready as he was, had no intention of going near the bathroom, he just continued his growl. izzy1969 looked at the bathroom door and then looked back at Beard. "OK, but you better back me up."

He began to walk very cautiously toward the bathroom door. Beard was alarmed at this, he barked at izzy1969 in protest. izzy1969 gestured to Beard to be quiet by placing his finger over his lips. Then he looked around. Just outside of the bathroom was a large bronze copy of the Eiffel Tower, about knee height with a solid black stone base. izzy1969 picked it up and held it above his head in both hands. He glanced back at Beard, who barked. "It's OK, Beard, there's no one inside, but if there is, I'm about to bash their head in."

Beard wanted to prevent his master from entering the bathroom. He made a pathetic attempt to reach him by crawling along on his stomach with tiny baby steps. He barked again, irritated at his own cowardice. Then he backed up against the wall. izzy1969 nodded and winked at Beard, then he kicked open the door and ran in. The bathroom was empty, the only presence was the cold.

"Holy shit." izzy1969 put the Eiffel Tower down and looked at Beard. "Holy shit," he said again, and exhaled. It was so cold he could see his breath. He smiled nervously, kind of scared but excited. "Can you see that?" he was amazed, he exhaled again. "Jesus, man, that is freakin' creepy, there *was* something in here, holy shit." Suddenly the cold was gone. izzy1969 held out his hand to feel the air. "Gone!" he exhaled again. "Gone, just like that."

He turned to look at Beard. Beard was fixed on izzy1969. "What's the matter? You look like you've seen a ghost," he chuckled disingenuously. "You don't like that gag, huh?"

He walked over to Beard and quickly rubbed Beard's head. Beard continued to stare at izzy1969. Some say that dogs have as many facial expressions as humans, and humans label similar expressions in dogs as indicating the same emotions as those of humans, so we feel we can read them and they can read us. But right now izzy1969 couldn't read Beard. *What the hell is wrong with you now?* he thought, but he didn't say it; this time it was izzy1969 who didn't want to say anything wrong.

Beard stared straight at him. He was still as if he wasn't even breathing, he looked calm and focused. izzy1969 decided to break the silence, and whispered, "Hey, bud, you OK? It's all over, you know."

Beard continued to look back at him, but at some point his expression had changed. izzy1969 had no idea when this had happened, as they hadn't broken eye contact. izzy1969 knew that look, it was the look of hatred. *All of a sudden my dog hates me, how did that happen?* izzy1969 reached out his hand to try and caress Beard.

"Come on, bud, what's—"

izzy1969s sincere attempt was savagely dealt with, as Beard

calmly and quickly opened his mouth and bit off the tip of his index

finger in one powerful hydraulic movement, a power far beyond the

normal capabilities of a dog, even a Rottweiler. He didn't chew,

growl, or make any sound at all. The whole moment was so relaxed

that izzy1969 couldn't quite believe it had actually happened.

Instead he snatched his hand back, briefly looked at it, and clasped it

under his other arm. He got up and urgently tried to walk to the door,

but he didn't get out of the kitchen. Beard trotted behind him and

took a small bite from his calf, which he let fall from his mouth.

izzy1969 fell to the floor, bellowing in agony. Beard recommenced

his matter-of-fact dining, turning to izzy1969's stomach,

accompanied by the sound of izzy1969's highly disturbing

protestations. izzy1969 began punching Beard as hard as he possibly

could. To get the most from each punch, he drew his arm back as far

as he could and released with all of his battered energy. He reached

above his head to the marble food island, nothing useful on top, but a

pen fell to the ground beside them, landing in a pool of blood on the

tiled floor.

Beard's teeth had a firm grip on izzy1969's ribcage and he was pulling back with all his might; steady sharp pulls. izzy1969 grabbed the slippery pen and stuck it firmly into Beard's neck. It had no effect. izzy1969 rolled onto his side and began pulling himself and Beard toward the hall phone, screaming for help. Suddenly, Beard stopped attacking. He just stopped, then after a few seconds, he began licking the face of his beloved master. Beard was agitated and whimpering, the pen sticking in his neck.

*

narcissus77. You're the highest bidder.

"OK, that's my lot, five hundred dollars." She checked the time remaining. "One minute, OK."

To the tune of "Hello, I Love You" by The Doors, she sang, "Leave the room, leave the room; otherwise you will bid again, bid again; otherwise you will bid again." She rushed away from the computer and from temptation. She walked casually into the bathroom, still humming her song. She reached for some mouthwash, poured some in the cap, and tossed it down her throat.

She began to gargle and swish. She walked toward the sink, leaning her hands on it as she swilled the liquid around, then looked up into the mirror. Looking back at her was a hideous reflection, old and disfigured, deformed, something void of life, dead, yet living. She spat out the mouthwash. It hit the mirror and trickled down the glass, disfiguring the reflection even further. She screamed hysterically in disbelief. She staggered backward, still transfixed on the reflected spectacle, shaking her head in denial.

She turned and tried to run back into the living room, but her tired old legs couldn't get her there. In fact, she could barely walk at all. She reached for her phone, but her hands had malformed into arthritic clubs, she couldn't even pick up the handset. Instead, it fell to the floor.

There was a thumping on her front door, then the muffled voice of her concerned neighbor Mr. Wei. "Sharon, Sharon! Are you OK? Let me in!" Sharon crawled toward the door. "Sharon, please let me in, I am calling the police." Sharon clambered up the door and managed to open it by twisting the knob with her wrists, and then she fell back down onto her back, exhausted.

Mr. Wei rushed in and knelt down, grabbing Sharon by the shoulders. She looked at him, too scared to speak. Her lips trembled, and she reached out and grabbed his lapels, her eyes searching him pleadingly.

"Sharon, what's wrong?" The question momentarily baffled Sharon, but then she noticed her hands, her young hands. Slowly, she sat up. Still looking at a bewildered Mr. Wei, she placed her hands on her face, and felt the contours of her young face. She rose to her feet, assisted by Mr. Wei. "Sharon, what happened?"

She turned to Mr. Wei. "Can you take me to the bathroom?"

"Sure, you gonna be sick?"

She didn't respond. They walked into the bathroom and faced the mirror. She saw a Chinese man holding the elbow of a beautiful Goth girl.

She turned to Mr. Wei and screamed into his chest, trembling. He didn't understand what had happened, and neither did she. He caressed her back.

"It's OK, Sharon. It's OK."

*

"Congratulations! You have won item 251789217."

Daniel Leyden smiled. "Hey! We won!" He tabbed back to the painting, and then turned to Patricia, who was asleep. He turned the empty champagne bottle upside down and placed it in the ice bucket, and then he laid his head on Patricia's legs. He mumbled, "happy anniversary." Daniel stared at the boy and the doll in the painting. He studied the hands behind the glass door. He drifted off to sleep. The screen eventually went dark as the screen saver came on, but it only lasted for a moment. The screen flickered back on the moment Daniel's eyes closed.

The Life Swapper

Captain O'Hara stood in the middle of a room that, if it wasn't for the ringing phone, could easily be in the late eighteenth century. O'Hara, a strapping, imposing man, one of the few on whom a grey comb-over actually looks good, has been in his precinct for years. His suit matched the walls, not the color, mind you, nothing to do with the color; they somehow just matched, the sort of phenomenon that happens over time in the same place.

He fanned himself with a cardboard page divider from a huge case file suspended on his left forearm. It wasn't hot, it was February, in Boston. The cold rain was pouring down the windows for the fifth day in a row. The fanning was to buy him time before he dished out the file. Normally he dished out case files like a Las Vegas dealer. This case, however, stuck to his fingers, and all the other detectives were busy trying to appear invisible. Not Detective Hector Gomez, though. He sat, one leg crossed over his knee and his hands clasped behind his head, slightly inclined in his ancient chair, as though he had just finished a meal and was onto a cigar and cognac.

Captain O'Hara was aware of the slight smirk on Gomez's face. "Captain, I know you're gonna give it to me. I don't know what you're waiting for." O'Hara just glanced at Gomez through the corner of his eye.

Detective McCabe got up and began to wrap up from the night shift. He chimed in, "Gomez, he's got something special there for you, I've never seen him hang onto one for so long."

O'Hara broke off fanning himself and looked at McCabe. "McCabe, take down the Christmas tree," he said, pointing at it without looking. "It's been up for too long."

Fellow officers looked at McCabe, their expressions all saying the same thing. McCabe responded to them, "I know, what a schmuck, right? Who but me would butt in when he's waving a file?" McCabe walked over to the tree and began to take off the decorations. In typical Boston PD style, the decorations were mug shots of wanted criminals. He threw some in the trash, and others he pinned to a cork-board, saying, "Caught yah, caught yah not, caught yah, caught yah not."

Gomez inquired again, "Cap?" The other night shift officers were making a quiet exit in case they picked up some shrapnel as McCabe did. O'Hara finally slammed the file down on Gomez's desk. Gomez just smiled. "I love the way you do this, it has a great effect, it really is showmanship." Gomez turned to McCabe, and said, "McCabe, the captain is good, huh? Wasted even, he could'a been a showman."

McCabe responded without turning from the tree. "He's OK, but he didn't say 'Ta-da' when he slammed the file down."

O'Hara sat on the corner of Gomez's desk, next to the large case file. "What season is it, Gomez?"

Gomez looked out the window "Well, it's mid-twenties outside, so I guess it's winter."

O'Hara widened his eyes. "And what comes after winter?"

Gomez leaned forward. "OK, Captain, you've put in a lot of effort, I'll set this one up for you. Why spring, of course, Captain."

"That's right, spring," said O'Hara. "So we'll be doing a wee bit of spring cleaning."

Gomez ran his finger over the file's dusty cover, and he flicked through the first few pages. O'Hara continued, "I'm re-assigning cases, fresh eyes and new blood. Best to do it now while we're quiet, the crooks don't like the cold, you know." He pointed at Gomez. "That's why Greenland has such a low crime rate, no one dares go outside. This was Manfreddi's, now it's yours, it's an FBI support case. I took off Manfreddi temporarily after his retirement until re-assignment, you've been with us six months now, I think it's a good fit."

Gomez looked at his dusty finger and showed it to the captain. "This literally has dust on it. He reads. 'The Life Swapper'?"

"I was going to take that one for myself but I said to myself, 'It's Gomez, it has "Gomez" written all over it. Yes, "The Life Swapper", that's what the press tagged it."

"Wait a minute!" Gomez shouted. "It says 1976 on here!"

"What about it?" O'Hara responded.

"Nineteen seventy-six!" Gomez insisted "Are you serious? I still had my paper route."

O'Hara pointed at the file. "If you'd take the trouble to read more than two lines, you'd see the last incident was in 1997, that's just three years ago. Besides, homicides committed in 1976 were largely the same as homicides committed today, just in bell-bottoms."

Detective Hershel Silvers entered the room. He took off his raincoat, shook off the water, and hung it on a coat rack. Then he took off his hat, revealing his dyed black hair. He had a pronounced hunch and a small, delicate frame.

O'Hara called out to Detective Silvers. "Hershey! Come over here." Silvers responded with a smile as he made his way over to O'Hara and Gomez.

"Morning, Cap', Gomez," said Silvers.

Gomez responded "Good morning! Good night, you mean. I need to get home and get some sleep, these all-night shifts are for the birds." Gomez removed the plaque with his name on it, opened a drawer, and replaced it with Silvers' plaque. He stood up.

Detective Silvers quipped, "Not birds, Gomez, they sleep at night."

"Wait a minute, Gomez, stay seated," said O'Hara. "Hersh, explain to Gomez here a little about the Life Swapper."

"WOW!" Detective Silvers crowed mockingly. "You got the Life Swapper? Captain, you're gonna spoil this boy, you sure he can handle it?"

Gomez feigned a smile. "Gee, Hersh, ooh, I can handle it, I can handle it."

Silvers leaned against an unoccupied desk and lit up a cigarette.

"OK, kid, it was a pretty big case. Still is really, the last incident was, wait a second…" Silvers glanced up, thinking, and Gomez interrupted.

"Nineteen ninety-seven. Please, Hersh, don't call me kid, or boy for that matter."

O'Hara walked back to his desk and slumped into his comfortable chair. "Yes, it was a big case, and as Hersh correctly says, it still is, but the press don't think so, and what drops from flavor of the month for the news agencies sometimes unfortunately drops off our desks. What? Don't look at me, well I'm not completely serious. In reality we just couldn't get anywhere, loads of ends, all of them dead."

Silvers took a long drag of his cigarette, and then gently stubbed it out against the back of the package and placed the butt inside. As he exhaled, he said, "The Life Swapper." He looked at the captain and then back at Gomez. "In May 1976 they found the mutilated remains of a Mr. Peabody. The detective in charge of the case was Manfreddi."

O'Hara raised his hand. "Excuse me, Hershey," he said, and turned to Gomez. "As I said, Francesco Manfreddi retired, just before you arrived. In fact, he was on the case until he retired last year. You'll need to go and pick his brains and get a knowledge transfer. He won't mind, he'd still love to nail it."

Silvers continued in a tone as if he was about to tell a joke— "a horse walks into a bar" kind of thing—"So, they arrive at the crime scene." Gomez flicked though the case file until he reached a file titled "Peabody"; inside there were multiple photographs of the crime scene showing the eyeless, mutilated body.

Silvers pointed at the file, "By the way, Peabody had no connection to the property, and the owner of the house was gone, and I don't mean on vacation, no one knew where he was, not family or neighbors. There was nothing there in that house but Peabody's mutilated corpse, and boy was he bad."

Gomez had seen some things in his career but this was another level of sick. "Yeah, I can see that. So, what, the owner of the house put Peabody's lights out and scrammed? No?"

O'Hara waved his finger and smiled. "If it were that simple, it wouldn't be on your desk now, would it? It also wouldn't be three inches thick. Another thing, there wasn't enough blood found at the scene for the amount of carnage, indicating he'd been killed somewhere else. That was true for all the victims, by the way."

Silvers nodded and O'Hara continued. "Naturally, an APB was put out on the owner, a Mr. Saxton."

Gomez read from the case file: "Sexton."

Silvers jumped back in. "So the manhunt was on for Saxton."

Gomez again corrected: "Sexton."

Silvers waved his hand dismissively. "Yeah, yeah, Sexton." He paused. "Where was I? That's right, they ran Peabody's prints through the system, he was listed as missing, had been missing for four years. Now here's where the fun starts. He also had an APB out on him. Manfreddi investigated the circumstances: Peabody was wanted for the murder of a fourteen-year-old girl, and she was found mutilated in his house in '72." Gomez located her in the files, and he stared at her picture. Even with her eyes missing it was clear she was looking at something, the last thing she saw maybe, her hands curled up in a failed attempt at self-protection. Silvers continued in a whisper, almost as if the information was too volatile to be said in a normal tone. "Anyway, even with the APB, there was no sign of Sexton. Then in 1978, he reappeared, he was found in a New York apartment, mutilated. The tenant was an old lady, a May something-or-other, who was missing. She turned up three years later, you get the idea."

Gomez read from the case log: "Nineteen seventy-six, '78, '81, '83, '86, '87, '90, '91, '94, '96, and '97."

Silvers added, "You can also include '72, that's when the young girl died. There's no pattern in the dates, but we're due another, that's a fact."

O'Hara grimaced. "Jesus, I hope not. In the case file is our permission of subcontract. Like I said it's a support case to the FBI, we partnered with them on this. The license is still good, it gets renewed every year."

Gomez smiled, "So I'm an FBI agent on this?"

O'Hara shook his head. "You'd like that, a chrome suit and sunglasses, but no, no you're not. It's part of inter-force collaboration, but it does give you power of arrest or interrogation across jurisdictions and so on. It's all written in the agreement, familiarize yourself with it"

"I get it," Gomez mumbled. "Anyway, all of these dates, it's a hell of a pattern."

"Hell is right," Silvers said. "The pattern is simple but chilling: a person goes missing, later gets found dead in a stranger's house, the owner is missing, that owner is later found dead in a stranger's house, that owner's missing and so on and so on, hence the handle 'the Life Swapper.' Then we had a visitor, a guy claiming he knew the location of the murders."

"Oh? Well … who?" Gomez asked.

Silvers chuckled. "The Great Apsland."

"The Great Apsland?" Gomez repeated.

The name seemed to trigger an alarm in O'Hara. "That asshole! Don't worry about it tonight, Gomez, Manfreddi can tell you all about him. Thanks, Hersh."

Silvers shook his cigarette packet against his ear. "My pleasure. Enjoy yourself, Gomez, I wish you the three Ps."

Gomez stood up and put on his jacket. He picked up the large case file and placed it in a leather briefcase. "'Three Ps'?" Gomez looked at both of them.

O'Hara smiled. "Patience, perseverance, and pluck. Now get some sleep, and don't show that file to your mother. How is she, by the way?"

"She's fine, thanks, I'll tell her you asked."

"You do that. Tonight was your last red-eye, tomorrow you are on this case full time. Go visit Manfreddi, get his details from Sally on your way out."

Gomez waved his hand. "Good night, good morning, good day," he said with a wink as he left.

Silvers tapped out his barely smoked cigarette from the packet and prepared to light it. "Nice kid."

Gomez called out from the hallway: "I heard that."

I'm Never Gonna Drink Again

The next day. The Leydens'. New Hampshire

Daniel and Patricia attempted to shower away their hangover. The main rule was to whisper. That was the golden rule, when you whisper any other activities and movements automatically fall in line and whisper too.

They made their way back to the living room.

"The scene of the crime," said Daniel. "Ah, the evidence!" He pointed at the empty champagne bottle. "We should bag it."

Both instantly focused on the screen. Daniel gave the laptop a nudge to wake it from the screen saver. Staring back at them was the boy and the doll. They sat down on the sofa gently. As they looked at the painting again, they were not as enthusiastic. They both felt a burden, a responsibility of sorts, it felt more like they had adopted, rather than purchased, the painting.

Patricia finally broke the silence. She looked at Daniel with conviction and began, "Daniel…"

Their children, Olivia and George, burst into the room and jumped all over Daniel and Patricia, a multitude of questions all asked at the same time in squeaky little voices.

Daniel held his head and grimaced. "Guys, please, my head, I have a mallet in my head."

"No you don't, Daddy," said four-year-old Olivia as she bounced on the sofa.

Patricia smiled. "No, honey, Daddy's just kidding. We stayed up a bit too late and now we feel a bit tired."

George, who was seven, helped his dad squeeze his head, while still bouncing. "Does this help, Dad?" he asked.

"You know, it actually does," replied a surprised Daniel. "It would be better without the bouncing, though." George grabbed Olivia's hand and they jumped down from the sofa and ran over to the breakfast table.

"Come on, Mom and Dad!" George shouted. "We've got to get to school!"

Patricia massaged her temples. "Now I remember why we never do this. Will you be OK dropping them off?"

Daniel waved his hand dismissively. "Yeah, I'm fine, it's poor Mr. Carter who's the real victim."

"What do you mean?" inquired Patricia.

"I'll be chiselling off his brace cement, and that stuff doesn't come off easily," Daniel replied. He held up his hands, pretending they were trembling.

Patricia laughed, and then held her head and grimaced. "Oh my head. Thank God Manuela's coming in today, I don't think I can do a thing, never mind clean this place."

Eventually, with hangovers on pause, the fragile parents finally sat down to breakfast. Patricia, however, got back up immediately, albeit reluctantly.

"Drat," she said as she remembered the children's lunches. She opened the refrigerator for some pre-prepared sandwiches which she placed into plastic lunch boxes. One was green with a picture of the Incredible Hulk punching a pavement until it cracked and the words, 'The Hulk Will Smash You.' The other featured Barney the Purple Dinosaur and the slogan, 'You're Super Dee Super!'

George reached toward the center of the table and grabbed a toy parrot. He held his spoon in his mouth, fumbled for the 'on' switch, took out the spoon and said, "Hi, Peter." The sound of tiny rotor mechanisms could be heard scratching inside the parrot, and then it turned from left to right, from nine o'clock to two o'clock, flapped its wings and replayed George's recorded voice: "Hi, Peter." The kids giggled, and Daniel and Patricia smiled. The parrot echoed the giggling, which made the kids laugh louder. Peter repeated this louder laughter, still turning from side to side, flapping his wings.

"OK, that's enough now," Daniel said firmly. The kids quieted down, but then Peter replayed Daniel "OK, that's enough now," and they all laughed. Patricia quickly picked up Peter and switched him off mid-flap before he had the chance to echo their laughter.

Olivia smiled, her dark eyebrows rose halfway up her forehead contrasting with her blonde, almost white hair. She said, "Peter's funny, huh, Mommy?"

Patricia caressed her head. "He sure is, honey."

A pensive George clattered his spoon against the ceramic cereal bowl as he scraped up the last bit of milk. "They should make a Hulk one."

"You mean, a Hulk parrot?" Patricia asked as she gulped some coffee.

An annoyed George replied, "No, not a Hulk one. The Hulk, not a green parrot, Mom, you can't have a Hulk parrot."

Daniel sided with his son, feigning disapproval. "Yeah. Patricia, get real, geez, you'll offend the Hulk! And then the Hulk will smash you, isn't that right, George?"

George rolled his eyes. "No, Dad, the Hulk's a good guy, he doesn't smash moms."

Daniel blew his daughter a kiss as she sat, amused at the conversation.

Patricia picked up the two lunch boxes. "OK, guys, let's pause this fascinating

debate till later. Lunches are ready, get your backpacks on now."

Daniel collected the lunch boxes from Patricia. He kissed her on the cheek, and then walked over to the children who were standing with their backs to Daniel, their backpacks on. He held out the Hulk and Barney boxes in front of them over their heads.

"George, which is yours?"

George smiled sarcastically. "Ha-ha, very funny, Dad."

Daniel chuckled silently. He packed the children's backpacks with their lunch boxes and ushered them to the door of the dining room. He turned to Patricia and made a Hulk crab body-building pose, growling.

Patricia leaned back on the kitchen counter, clasping her hot coffee, which warmed both hands. She smiled, "I love you, too."

The door closed, the three voices became muffled, the deeper voice saying something and the small voices responding, and then laughing. Patricia smiled again. She heard the clunk of the car doors, the familiar sound of the ignition and the engine, the reverse, the pause, and then the final sound of the car moving off, the sound becoming quieter and quieter until they were gone. She looked at her watch: eight-fifteen.

Patricia glanced over at the coffee table and saw the back of the laptop. She wandered over, still clasping her hot coffee. The screen was blank. She tapped the space bar and the painting appeared. She stared deeply into the eyes of the boy and studied the surroundings intensely. The wooden frame of the door, and the searching hands suspended behind the dark windows. The empty dark eye sockets of the doll stared back at Patricia. This sent a physical chill all through her body, but she could not break herself away. She sipped some coffee and instantly spat the coffee back into the cup. It was stone cold. She touched the ceramic sides of the cup. There was no doubt; the cup that moments ago warmed her hands was now completely cold. She stared back at the doll as she heard the sound of a key in the door.

"Ma'am, ma'am," called an inquiring voice.

"Manuela?" asked Patricia.

Manuela put down two bags of groceries in the hallway and leaned on the door frame. "It's so cold out there, not like my hot motherland, this Manchester, it's so cold. Oh, my poor hands, it's so nice and warm in here."

Manuela was confused by the surprise in Patricia's greeting, she always arrived at this time and couldn't understand why Patricia was so surprised to see her. Manuela wiped the condensation from her glasses.

"Did Daniel ask you to come early?" Patricia asked.

Manuela was even more confused. "Ma'am? Early?"

Patricia looked at her watch. It was eleven o'clock. Patricia looked back at Manuela to respond but she found herself lost for words. Manuela picked up the bags again. "I'll go put these things away."

Patricia turned sharply and looked back at the screen. She gave her watch one more glance and confirmed the time on the laptop clock, aware she was avoiding the doll's eyeless stare.

Gomez's House

Using his right hand, Gomez stabbed one of his two fried eggs with a bit of toast. In his left hand, he held the crime scene photograph of the first victim. Eyes missing and multiple lacerations. He picked up more pictures, each as horrific as the next, all mutilated, of all ages and sexes, all with their eyes missing. He continued to stab his eggs.

The phone rang. Gomez's mother broke away from the small book she was reading, an Italian book of puzzles called *Enigmistica*. She peered over her glasses at an engrossed Gomez, busy multitasking. Then she clipped her pen to the book's cover, got up from the table, and walked to the phone, inadvertently bringing her book with her. The phone was an old rotary phone of ivory-colored plastic. It sat on a doily on a tall, slim phone table. It looked like a king on throne; a shrine calling back to the days when the phone demanded a shrine. It was accompanied by an eclectic assortment of unrelated objects: a pewter ashtray (Gomez's father was a smoker. Maybe that's what killed him. The doctors could never say for sure where the cancer started), an unopened plastic hexagonal box of toothpicks, dating back to the 1950's when everything was over-engineered even disposable items, it featuring a round swivel top that allowed you to choose only one toothpick at a time. There was a nail clipper, a small plastic donkey with a faded Mexican rider on top, and a small metallic green die-cast toy sports car with an orange windshield, in played-with condition, none of which could assist any type of call. Underneath the table was a drawer, and then a long cavity designed to hold a tall vase of flowers. Instead there was a tiny forgotten cactus at the bottom, using none of this intentionally designed space, stubbornly defying the balance. If it could talk, it would have said "What?"

Mrs. Gomez turned to her son. "Hector, it's for you, it's the precinct."

Gomez stood up and walked over to the phone. He noticed the book and smiled.

"*Enigmistica*, Ma, you've been reading those for twenty years, they're Italian, you're not even Italian!"

His mother sat back down and re-opened her book.

"I don't like the Spanish ones; the spot-the-difference bit is always too easy. Anyway, *io capisco molto bene l'Italiano, non ti preoccupare*."

Her son smiled and he picked up the phone. "Detective Gomez." He listened and then put a hand over the speaker. "Ma, can you get me a pen and paper?"

His mother got back up and passed him her book and pen, he wrote down an

address on the cover. It was Manfreddi's address. He wrapped up the call. "Thanks, Sally."

He saw his mother looking at the name. "Ma, he was on the case I'm now assigned to, I'm gonna go and talk to him."

Mrs. Gomez touched her son's arm. "But why do you have to do this job?" Gomez walked back to the table. "Oh not this again, Ma."

"Yes, this again," Mrs. Gomez replied as she followed him to the table. "I already lost your father, I don't need to lose you too."

Gomez turned to his Mother. "Ma, like I've said a hundred times, I'm not walking a beat, the job really isn't as dangerous as you think."

Mrs. Gomez leaned around her son and picked up a crime scene photo of one of the victims. A black woman, with no eyes, nose, or fingers. "OK, so you're telling me you want to catch the person who did this, and I mustn't worry, huh?"

Gomez gently held his mother's face and smiled. "Ma, what am I gonna do about you?"

Delivery

Patricia was running over the morning's strange events as she made some tea. Knocks and clonks could be heard in the hallway as Manuela was busy dusting the furniture.

The doorbell rang. Manuela placed her duster under her arm and walked over to the door. She peered out through the peephole, but she couldn't see anyone. She opened the door but there was no one there. Then she heard the sound of a car engine, which made her turn in its direction, she saw a run-down compact car drive off briskly. As she was about to close the door, she realized that a package was lying against the wall beside the door. She bent down to pick up the package and as she did so, she heard a shrill, child-like wailing, the sound grabbing her stomach in an ice fingered clench. She turned to see two cats standing off in the front yard, and muttered to herself, "blasted cats, you scare me half to death."

She half ran down the porch steps to scare them off, they ran away in opposite directions. Out of breath, she picked up the package, brought it back into the house, and walked into the kitchen.

Patricia asked, "Who was it?"

"Nobody, just this," Manuela responded.

Patricia paused. "It must be the painting." She paused again and looked at Manuela. Manuela handed the package over to Patricia, who began to tear off the brown paper. "That was quick, we only bought it last night." She looked at the plain wrapping paper. "No stamps, they must have hand-delivered it."

"Ah, yes, I saw an old car drive away quickly," Manuela said. Patricia finished tearing off all of the wrapping paper and gently held the painting at arm's length. She walked over to a cabinet and placed the painting upon it. She walked backward, looking at the painting.

Manuela was horrified. She recoiled, placing her hand on her chest. Then she turned to Patricia and asked, "ma'am, you bought this?"

Patricia reluctantly responded to the uncomfortable question. "Yes, well, Daniel and I."

Manuela was incapable of reading her discomfort, she insisted, with full blameless innocence, "Why?"

Patricia felt she had to make a stand. "Don't you like it?"

Manuela, her hand still on her chest, answered, "No. No, I don't like this, ma'am, now I see why the car sped away." She paused to look at it again. "Where are you going to put it?" she enquired with trepidation.

"Outside my room in the landing, above the telephone," Patricia responded. "At least it won't scare the kids there."

"I don't think they will ever come to your room again," Manuela gibed.

At this, Patricia re-asserted her confident stance. "Great, no more early morning wake-ups then. Can you put it there now? Just replace that old print that's there."

Manuela reluctantly proceeded to bring the painting upstairs. She arrived at the landing, took down the print, and placed the new painting upon the hook. She stood back and studied the painting. She looked deeply into the eyes of the boy, and then the doll. Manuela was captivated by the image. Slowly, she blessed herself.

Patricia watched Manuela from the landing below. Manuela stared deeply into the painting. A slight almost imperceptible squint of Manuela's eyes. It seemed as though she was staring at a distant object, not something painted on the canvas. She was looking far away, and she saw something, or she felt something, she could not focus precisely on whatever it was, yet whatever it was grew nearer, the almost-imperceptible squint was now gone as whatever she saw, or felt, was no longer far away.

"Manuela!" Patricia snapped.

Manuela jumped, she looked down the stairs at Patricia. "ma'am, you startled me."

Patricia smiled. "Sorry, but you were staring so hard at the painting."

Manuela looked at Patricia intensely. "ma'am." She looked at the painting again, and then back down at Patricia. "ma'am, these … are not children of the Lord."

Patricia heard every word. She wrangled her emotions in line and replied, "Oh, Manuela, you're too easily spooked, you spooked yourself! That's what you get for staring too hard at them."

Manuela didn't acknowledge the comment. "I'll get my things and go home now, it's time."

Patricia walked up the stairs to the landing and looked at the picture. She giggled nervously, mumbling to herself how silly Manuela was.

The One That Got Away

Sitting at a dining table, the case files spread out, Ex-detective Manfreddi and Gomez flicked through the papers.

"'The Life Swapper,' the one that got away, you'll have one too," Manfreddi said.

"Don't I know it," responded Gomez. "Very probably the Life Swapper. And you never found anything to tie the murders together? I mean, anything? Regardless of what?"

Manfreddi shook his head and chuckled. "One day, one day though, I had a break. A man walks into the office looking for *me*. He says he knows where the victims were killed. So—and this was eight years into the case—so I welcome him, sit him in my chair. The Captain even joined us, so did O'Hara, he was just one of us in those days, not a Captain yet. In fact we had half the officers on duty sitting around, listening to his every word."

"Was this the 'Great Apsland'?" inquired Gomez, making air quotes.

"Ah, I see the boys told you about him. Yes, Dyson Von Bilbow Apsland, a name you can't easily forget. Originally a native of Germany, he was a parapsychologist, that's the first time I'd ever heard the word. It was the first time any of us had ever heard the word. So he says, 'Your victims were not killed where they were found.' Well, we almost fell off our chairs, because we and CSI had concluded that already—not enough blood found at the locations and zero blood splatter—but we hadn't let on to the press, so how he knew was of interest to us. So Apsland explained further, he described the victims, the mutilation and—" he placed his index finger in his mouth and made a popping sound—"eyes out."

"So what? That part was in the newspapers, right?" said Gomez.

"Yes, so we didn't pay any attention to his description of the mutilation; it was his insistence that they were murdered elsewhere that hooked us. But he struggled to name a location. We even brought in a special military unit, who threw some co-ordinates at Apsland, it was based on some research they had been doing into, would you believe, mind travel. Anyway, it didn't work. When pushed, Apsland reluctantly shared his reason for not being able to give a location."

An intrigued Gomez asked, "Which was?"

Manfreddi smiled. "This is where Apsland lost his audience." He sighed. "Apsland claimed that he couldn't 'feel' the location was of this world. He said whenever he went into a trance to look for it, he was always taken outside of, as he put it, 'our realm'."

"I see," said Gomez.

Manfreddi looked at him with a slight smirk. "No you don't. Neither did I, and the captain, wow, he virtually threw Apsland out of the office. I'll give Apsland one thing, he was passionate about this case. It'd be worth you contacting him. His address is in the notes, if he's still there."

Beddie-byes

The family stood on the landing, looking at the picture.

"So, what do you think, kids?" asked a goading Daniel.

"They're creepy, Dad," said George.

Olivia wasn't happy either. "The doll doesn't have eyes, dolls have eyes, you see? Look at Alice."

Olivia held up her doll. "She has eyes. That dolly is silly, I don't like her."

Patricia looked at Daniel. "There you go." She ushered the kids to their room. "OK, off to bed, come on."

It was a still night; the snow outside muffled any external sounds. Just the occasional exchange of dogs barking could be heard in the distance.

Two O'clock in the morning.

Daniel was in a deep sleep, however he became aware of something, he slowly opened his eyes. In the darkness, he saw the silhouettes of George and Olivia, holding hands. He mumbled, half-asleep "Kids, what? You can't sleep? School tomorrow, remember?"

His eyes closed, and then reopened them, they were still standing there. "Kids, I said go to bed!"

He looked to his wife but she was not in the bed.

Patricia called, "Daniel, who are you talking to?"

"Where are you?" he responded instantly, trying not to sound too alarmed.

Patricia replied, "I'm in the kids' room, they couldn't sleep."

Daniel scrambled to switch on the bedside light. He walked into the children's room, where Patricia lay on the floor in a blanket tangled between the children who were fast asleep. Patricia mouthed the word, "What?" to Daniel. He mouthed back, "It's OK."

He returned to the bedroom, pausing momentarily by the painting before continuing inside.

Patricia called in a whisper, "Daniel, can you switch your light off or close the door?

Daniel whispered back, "Are you gonna come back to bed?"

"I don't think so," Patricia said.

"Then no," Daniel responded firmly, and placed a T-shirt over his eyes.

The Great Apsland

Gomez rang the doorbell of the run-down apartment. A few moments later, the door partially opened, a tall man with strong, noble features, black graying hair and moustache appeared in the gap. Gomez displayed his badge. "Good morning, sir, my name is Detective Hector Gomez from Boston South Side, Homicide division."

Apsland contemplated his visitor with a stony gaze. Gomez, unsure how to react, was about to explain again why he was there, but then Apsland smiled graciously and invited Gomez inside. "Homicide, you say, please come in."

Gomez stepped into the apartment. It was full of plants and stuffed woodland animals and was lit by a collection of old lava lamps, casting an ever-changing lighting effect from dark blue to blood red. Apsland guided Gomez to his kitchen. "Can I offer you some tea or coffee?"

A grateful Gomez rubbed his hands together. "Coffee would be nice, thanks, it's so cold out there." Apsland began to prepare the coffee.

"I guess you're wondering why I'm here? Gomez chirped energetically.

Apsland smiled. "Not at all, I know why you're here. You're here to talk to me about the Life Swapper."

Gomez was surprised. "That's correct. How did you guess?"

Apsland pointed a long finger. "A detective doesn't carry a bag unless he is carrying a case file, and by the look of that bulging satchel, it's a big case. I worked with the Boston PD briefly on the Life Swapper, itself a big case, hence you are here for that. How am I doing?"

"Very impressive," nodded Gomez.

Apsland chuckled disingenuously. "Yes, that, and the fact that Manfreddi called me."

Gomez smiled. "Just when I was about to compare you to the legendary Sherlock Holmes."

Apsland changed his attitude like a bat changes direction and blurted out,

"Be warned, mind you, should one whisper of ridicule or any hint of sarcasm come from your person, you will be asked to leave. I had all that the last time I worked with your pals."

Gomez could see Apsland was not joking. "You have my word."

Apsland handed Gomez his coffee, and they both sat down at a large dining table. Gomez spilled out the contents of the case on the table.

He took a sip of coffee. "So what did you deduce from the crime scene photos when you went through them with Manfreddi?"

"That the victims did not die where they were photographed. And I didn't deduce, I felt it."

"I heard the captain was piss … uh, excuse me, kinda annoyed that you thought the location was 'not of this Earth'."

"Correct. I suppose in retrospect I cannot blame him for being angry, he was frustrated with me. *I* was frustrated with me, I knew, know the location, but what to do about it? You know my view, it's 'not of this earth,' so what do we do?"

Gomez could only respond, "Yeah, we can't get a cab, that's for sure." He immediately corrected himself. "Uh, I mean, agreed, what do we do about it?"

Apsland studied Gomez. Gomez, feeling it, studied Apsland back. Apsland folded his arms. "You're now wondering what I can do for you?"

Gomez nursed his coffee. "Yes, sir, I guess I am."

Apsland clasped his hands together. "Detectives always go with their gut. Well, us spiritual types we go with our Spirit. There is a residual energy from these crimes and it does not lead me to search on this earth for the culprit, as I know the hand that took these victims lives is not of this world." He waited for a response, but Gomez remained silent. "Detective Gomez, what do you want from me?"

"Help," Gomez said honestly. "I, and this case, need help."

"Then you must open your mind. You do that and we might have a chance."

"You mean, like imagine one hand clapping?" Gomez asked.

Apsland glanced suspiciously at Gomez. "Hmm, even though I feel you are making fun of me, yes, exactly! Imagine one hand clapping."

Gomez smiled. "I'm not making fun. OK you've got a deal, when can you start?"

"I started when Manfreddi called me," answered Apsland.

Phone Call

A week later.

Patricia was on the phone with a Cynthia, it was a mother's daytime call. Patricia hated them, and so did Cynthia, as they both had to pretend they were friends. Nevertheless, they persisted, as it was the only way to plan birthday parties and play dates.

Patricia asked, "Cynth! Are your kids there with you?"

"No, they're at school, why?"

"Nothing," said Patricia. "Just I thought I could hear a kid crying. I thought it must be Rory."

"But there *was* a child crying," Cynthia said quickly. "I thought it was George."

"No, no," said Patricia. "They're at school too. In fact, I have to go and pick them up soon, hold on a second."

Patricia cupped the phone and shouted to Manuela.

"Manuela, are you on the phone?"

A delayed response muted up through the floor boards. "No, ma'am, I am in laundry room."

"Cynth, I'll call you back." Without waiting for acknowledgement, Patricia hung up the phone and walked into the hallway. The hall phone was on its rest. She tentatively walked upstairs to the bedroom landing, and looked at the phone underneath the painting. The receiver was off the hook, hanging from its coil, slowly swinging. She placed it back on the base and it immediately started to ring, causing Patricia to shriek. She tentatively picked it up.

"Cynth?" asked Patricia nervously.

"Hi, uh, no this is Henrietta Johnson at the nursery."

"Oh. Hello, Mrs. Johnson."

Patricia paused and automatically asked the question every parent asks when they receive a call from the school or nursery. "Is everything OK?"

"Oh don't be alarmed, I just wondered if you or Dr. Leyden could swing by to talk with me when you pick Olivia and George up from school today?"

Patricia wasn't convinced of Mrs. Johnson's sincerity. "Yeah, sure. Are you sure everything is OK?"

The principal confirmed and at the same time reaffirmed the insincerity. "Absolutely! I just wanted to have a quick chat, nothing to be alarmed about."

"OK, we'll be in today." Patricia hung up the phone and stared pensively at the painting.

The Nursery

Ms Joyce was flicking through Olivia's artwork while the principal, Patricia, and Daniel watched. Miss Joyce always looked concerned; it was just her expression, so much so, that when she received a birthday present last year, everyone thought she didn't like it. This made it difficult for Patricia to see where she was going with this.

"Again nice, trees, dog, house, this one is after we went to the museum, so dinosaurs, she's very talented, great use of colors. Family, very nice, all smiling, and then this:" Miss Joyce stopped on a drawing in red crayon of a group of people lying on a red floor with black holes for eyes.

Daniel involuntarily cried, "Holy mackerel!" and snatched the picture from Miss Joyce.

"This is what we wanted you to see." Miss Joyce said.

"Are you saying our four-year-old Olivia drew this?"

"Yes she did, Dr. Leyden."

"But, but I don't understand. It's horrible. Why?" asked Patricia.

"We were hoping you might be able to shed some light on that. We wouldn't even have raised the issue if the image wasn't so disturbing," said Mrs. Johnson.

Daniel held the drawing in both hands. "But how? Are you sure she drew this? It's not just a question of its ugliness, but this is not a drawing from the hand of a four year old. It's far too mature, look at her other stuff; no, no she must have picked it up from somewhere."

Miss Joyce and Mrs. Johnson exchanged a knowing glance, which was spotted by Patricia, adding an extra knot in her stomach.

Miss Joyce said, "Dr. Leyden, I watched her draw it myself. I asked her what it was and she said it was a tree and a cat."

"Tree and a cat!? What!" repeated a bemused Daniel.

Mrs. Johnson interjected. "Miss Joyce and I agree that Olivia wasn't aware of what she drew even as she did so."

"Miss Joyce, can you call her in please?" asked Patricia. Miss Joyce left the room, leaving Daniel, Patricia, and Mrs. Johnson to ponder in silence. No attempt at deflective banter took place, it would have been absurd, so they just stood in silence. That is until Mrs. Johnson asked the question she had been holding pressed behind her lips.

"How are things at home?"

Daniel, holding the offending drawing, couldn't help feeling like he was holding a dead rat. "They're fine thanks, absolutely fine."

Miss Joyce came back with Olivia, who ran happily to her mother's arms.

"Hi Mommy, hi Daddy."

"Hi sweetheart," said Daniel. "Did you have a nice day?"

"I sure did," said Olivia.

Patricia leaned over so she was at eye level with Olivia. "Miss Joyce says you made a nice picture for us?"

Olivia turned and looked through her art folder. "I did yes, and it's very beautiful, there is a cat and a tree, and I think a flower ... oh, where is it, Miss Joyce?"

Miss Joyce whispered, "She still thinks she's drawn it, it's really strange."

Daniel handed Olivia her picture. "Did you draw this, honey?"

"Yuck! Don't be so silly Daddy, why would I draw those scary people?"

"Why indeed?" mumbled Patricia as she made eye contact with Daniel.

*

The fresh air that met them on exiting the school was blessed. They felt like they were out on bail. George had joined them, and they all marched toward their car. No explanations could be given by either side. They didn't look back at the school but were certain Miss Joyce and Mrs. Johnson were looking at them.

"Why are you both being so weird?" asked George in an uncomfortably loud voice. When they ignored him, he persisted. "Hello?"

They both held out until they were in the sanctuary of their car. Only when George and Olivia were suitably engrossed in their own chatter did Patricia dare to speak, and even then she whispered.

"Daniel, you know, today something else weird happened."

"What's that?"

Patricia looked into the rear view mirror to check on the children. George was busy stealthily opening a candy bar, he looked up to meet Patricia's reflected disapproving eyes. "George, put that down, no eating, you'll be in the pool in ten minutes." She reached back and took the bar from him, which prompted Olivia to smugly remind him that she had told him so. Patricia turned back to Daniel.

"I was on the phone with Cynthia today." She glanced back in the mirror to confirm the children weren't listening. "During the call, I heard crying, a child's crying. I thought it was Rory. I asked Cynthia, and she thought it was one of ours, so we both heard it."

Daniel shrugged. "A crossed line?"

Patricia paused. She leaned over and whispered.

"Then I checked the hall phone, it was on the receiver, but when I went up to check the other phone, it was off the hook and swinging."

Unable to offer an explanation, Daniel was delighted to see the swimming pool's parking lot come into view "We're here."

Patricia and the children exited the car. Daniel rolled down the window, and Patricia placed her hand on the open frame. "Do you want to come in?"

Daniel looked at his watch. "I can't, I have to finish a presentation for a dental seminar. I'll be at home, just call me when you're almost ready to leave."

"Don't worry," Patricia said, and waved. "Cynthia will drop us off." She smiled glumly. "Ciao."

Pressure at the Leyden's House

It was a bright crisp Saturday mid-morning. The Leydens had invited some friends for lunch, it was a spur of the moment thing, probably done subconsciously to attempt to relieve some of the anxiety they had experienced over the nursery visit. Cynthia and her Son Rory, Penny, Olivia's nursery friend and her Mother, there was Tom and Brandon, Daniels high school friends, and Patricia's uncle Geoff. George held his shiny silver UASF Corsair like a javelin as he flew it through the hallway, hot on the tail of Mitsubishi Zero Pilot and George's best friend, Rory. They raced through the air in an intense dogfight to the death, accompanied by superb sound effects, sound effects only kids can indulge in without the restrictions of self-consciousness that (sober) adults are burdened with. They blasted through the air, skilfully dodging huge adults, and making one masterful descent under a silver tray held in the suspended hand of Cynthia.

"Whoa! Hey! Be careful, you two."

Rory, being shorter than George, was always going to be vulnerable to a dive attack from an arm held at least two inches higher, which was equivalent to a two-hundred-foot advantage for George in the air.

Cynthia placed the long tray on the marble-topped kitchen island. "Is this the one?"

Patricia nodded, "Yes honey." She held out a glass of white wine to Cynthia and Penny's Mother.

"Ooh, we're starting early, huh?" said Cynthia, who took the glass eagerly. Penny's Mother intentionally waited a beat before taking hers.

"Just to wet your whistle." Said Patricia.

"Moh-ho-ho-ho-homeee," cried Olivia, as she ran up to Patricia's legs.

"What is it, honey?" Patricia bent down to Olivia, who was pouting and looked very tragic.

"Penny said her doll would be the teacher, but *I* thought of the game and my doll Alice is the teacher."

"That isn't true!" snapped a little voice from the door.

"Penny," said her mother, giving her a sharp look. "Is it?"

"Well, we both thought of it at the same time," Penny responded resolutely.

Olivia shook her head. Patricia glanced at Penny's mother and squinted her eyes in a smile, then she looked back at Olivia as she wiped the tears from her soft cheeks. "OK, I have an idea." Patricia turned Olivia around to face Penny, who was clinging to the protection of the door frame. "Why can't there be two teachers?"

Olivia beamed from ear to ear and immediately ran toward an equally beaming Penny. *Peace in our time*, thought Patricia.

Patricia looked at her fingernails and then at Penny's mother. "You're a lawyer, how was that for negotiation?"

Penny's mother grasped Patricia's wrist. "Supermom, You-are-wasted." They clinked glasses. "I'll bring you in to assist me for Herman vs. Herman."

"Is that still going on?" said Cynthia

"You bet, everything's agreed, house, child support, alimony, everything but one thing." Penny's mother sniggered into her glass, inducing similar sniggers from Patricia and Cynthia.

"What?" asked an impatient, grinning Cynthia.

"He wants her underwear."

"What?" screamed Patricia, they all broke into laughter.

"I'm not kidding," continued Penny's mother. "He said he bought it, and it'll remind him of her. Mrs. Herman said it's macabre. Negotiate that one, Patricia."

Patricia pondered for a brief moment, then held up her finger

"I've got it! I'd suggest she can have his underwear, how's that?"

*

Daniel stood at the top of the stairs like a curator in a museum. "And the guy who listed it even took pictures of these things he said were coming out of the painting."

"So, Daniel?" asked Tom, stroking his dyed beard (the color looks natural, but it's too uniform, a dead giveaway), "do you believe *it is* cursed?"

"Argh," Daniel waved his hand dismissively. "Nah, it's just fun, a bit of fun." He looked down the stairs and whispered, "Patricia doesn't like it, though." He looked back at the painting. "But *I* do.

Anyway, it's a great conversation piece, you see! Look at us, conversing." They chuckled.

Brandon, they called him 'street lamp' at school, very bright and very tall, subconsciously adopted the top portion of the pose of Auguste Rodin's famous thinker as he contemplated. Brandon was intimidatingly clever, having made all of his money in banking software. He seemed to know everything, if Brandon told you your mother used to be a stripper in a Shanghai club called 'Bottoms Up', you'd instantly reply in a dazed whisper: 'I never knew … I never knew.' However, thankfully, for the group, he had no such news. Instead he simply said, "This painting looks to me as if it has a function."

"Yeah, to be looked at." Tom, smiling clumsily, looked at them both for acknowledgment of his witty remark. He looked left to Daniel and right to Brandon, with sharp movements like a chicken. But the backdrop to his head twitching was silence. Tom gave up the chase for his joke as he too finally realized Brandon's observation did indeed deserve some thought.

"What do you mean?" asked Daniel.

"I'm not sure, but this wasn't painted just for the sake of art, or for any of usual motivations."

"What are *they*?" asked Daniel.

"For me, *for me*, you understand, the motivations are adoration, redemption, exorcism, or a combination"

"Then what was this painted for?"

Brandon looked at Daniel. "I can only see one thing."

Tom toyed nervously with his empty beer bottle as he played the role of a ping-pong spectator to this conversation.

"Well, what?" asked Daniel.

Brandon pointed his finger so it was millimetres from the painting. "Want. This *wants* something."

"Jesus, Brandon!" Tom said in a berating tone. "You're the science-type here, and you're sounding like Nostradamus or Houdini. You don't believe in all that stuff, do you?"

"No Bryan, and by the way, I'm not quite sure where Nostradamus or Houdini come in. But, no, no I don't believe in such things. I mean purely from a cold logical perspective. I think this was painted to get something."

"Yeah, money." Again no one laughed. Tom looked at them both, and shook his head in resignation. "Not funny, huh? Ah, Jesus, you guys are hard work, I'm going downstairs for another beer."

Daniel said, "No, not funny, but the Houdini and Nostradamus reference was."

*

The table was set and most of the Leydens' guests had found themselves drifting to it. Patricia turned down the hob so the pressure cooker only made a tiny hiss. Her work was done. Just as well, the wine had started to hit. She wasn't worried though, her stomach would soon be full and even her out.

Uncle Geoff had missed the painting discussion as he had been hanging out with the kids. He was busy showing George and Rory a hand trick with a deck of cards. The table finally had all of the guests seated.

Daniel sat at the head of table, but then he immediately stood up, champagne flute in hand. "Thank you all for coming. I hope you like the appetizers, ravioli di cinghiale al tartufo." The group dug in.

"So what actually is this, Daniel?" asked Uncle Geoff.

"It's wild boar in truffle," replied Penny's mother.

"Ah, that's why I've never had it before," said Uncle Geoff. "Only lawyers and orthodontists can afford it."

"Daddy, Daddy," George raised his fork in the air as if asking his teacher at school for permission to speak.

"George? What's up?"

"Daddy, can you do that trick with the glass?"

Daniel smiled, and he took a sip of his Prosecco.

"What trick is that, Daniel?" asked Cynthia.

Patricia laughed. "It's where he pours wine in a glass and makes it disappear."

Daniel gave his wife a toothy grin. "Well, my evil wife is half right." He took a wine glass and half-filled it with a fresh glass of white wine. "I'm moving onto wine now, anyway." He dipped his finger in the wine and began to steadily rub the rim. The adults pretended to be amazed, and the kids were amazed as a clear note hummed from his glass. The adults adored the expressions on the children's faces. Olivia, in particular, was spellbound.

"Daddy let me try? Let me?" She dipped her finger in her water and tried to rub the rim of her plastic cup.

"No, gorgeous," Uncle Geoff placed his wine glass in front of her and filled it halfway with water. "Now try."

Olivia had the floor. She again dipped her index finger in the water and then began to rub the rim. Sure enough, after a few unsteady navigations, a faint hum could be heard. It disappeared as she derailed, and then it came back loud and sharp each time she was back on target. Olivia was stunned, her eyes wide and mouth open, to the delight of the audience. Patricia instigated a round of applause. The sound of the humming was loud. In fact, it became louder.

"What?" murmured a surprised Brandon as he looked around the table. Everyone looked perplexed. The applause began to peter out. The sound of the humming was louder than that trick had ever produced at any dinner party, ever.

"OK, honey, that's enough," said Patricia firmly. Olivia, Penny, and the two boys were both frozen in amazement. When you're a kid, you think everything's possible, when you're an adult you know everything's not, and this was evident in the contrasting expressions of the amazed children to those of the horrified adults. Olivia continued to rub the rim of the glass.

"That's enough, I said!" snapped Patricia.

Olivia immediately lifted her finger with a jerk, almost as if Patricia's command had produced an electric shock jolting Olivia's finger off.

But the sound continued strong and clear. Patricia stood up. Even the kids knew this wasn't right. Geoff instinctively put his arm in front of Olivia, between her and the glass. They all stared at this affront to the given laws of science as it rang unforgivingly. It began to vibrate intensely, finally reaching a maximum at which the stresses produced could not be sustained. It exploded, and it exploded at exactly the same moment as the pressure cooker. The room was instantly engulfed in steam, creating a complete whiteout.

The screams of the children were met with the cries of the women, which were met with the yells of the men. Through it all, the only words that made sense were the same word said twice: "Outside, outside."

The beautifully prepared table of crystal glasses and silverware made its way audibly to the floor as the panic to get to the door had dragged the table cloth off.

"I've got Olivia, honey." Said Daniel.

"George, George!" shouted Patricia into the blindness. She clamoured around awkwardly searching, she reached down. "Ah, there you are, give me your hand."

She made her way to the open door.

"George, what are you doing?" Patricia cried angrily.

"What's wrong?" shouted Daniel from outside.

"Ah, you're hurting me, stop that, we have to go outside," said Patricia.

"Patricia, what's wrong?" insisted Daniel.

Patricia waved away some of the steam from her face. Outside she could see that the whole group, including George, were already on the grass on the foot of the porch. The small hand released its nails from her palm and disappeared back into the mist.

Daniel had never heard Patricia scream, not even as a joke. In fact, for a few microseconds, it didn't even occur to him it was her making this sound. Once he did, he bolted to her and pulled her down the porch steps onto the grass. Patricia looked at each of them, and she trembled and shook.

"My God," said Cynthia. "What happened?"

"It's only venison, Patricia," joked Tom.

"Nice try, Tom," said Brandon discreetly. "What happened, Patricia?"

Patricia looked at the children, whom all looked concerned. As any good mother would, she smiled, albeit a smile fighting quivering lips, and chuckled.

"You're right, Tom, it's only venison." The group laughed sympathetically as some of them made their way back into the house waving there hands around to disperse the steam, leaving Patricia, Daniel, Bryan, and Brandon to pick over the events.

"Daniel?" asked Patricia.

Daniel turned around. "Yes, honey?"

Brandon asked again, "Patricia, what happened?"

Patricia was hesitant. She didn't want to bring this up with Daniel in front of the guests. But Brandon insisted.

"Brandon," said Daniel. "Don't insist, she'll say something weird happened."

Patricia was about to turn into a pit bull, but Tom noticed this and came to her rescue. "What on Earth are you talking about, Daniel? Something weird *did* happen."

"What, the glass?" Daniel shrugged.

"You're damn right, the glass."

"That could have been anything."

"What? What the hell could it have been? I've never seen anything like that, not even at midnight on Saint Patrick's Day, the goddamn glass breaking into bits, the thing humming and crying away there even though Olivia took off her finger. You're damn right it's weird, and then your pot exploding." Tom paused, no counter-argument was offered, so he continued. "Even Brandon here will say it's weird, and he has as much emotion as a calculator, no offense, Brandon."

"I agree, it was weird, no question about that." said Brandon, to Tom's contentment. "But that doesn't mean it is without an explanation. For example, if the pressure cooker was about to explode, it is possible, at least maybe, that the steam escaping at such intensity before the explosion might have resulted in high frequency sounds, sounds that are inaudible to us, causing the glass to hum. You know, I guess you could call it the soprano principle. We've all seen what they can do to a crystal glass."

"There you go," claimed Daniel, insisting upon his vindication. "That's the explanation."

"No, no," rebuked Brandon. "It's merely a suggestion. And it still doesn't explain why Patricia screamed at the door."

Patricia folded her arms and looked at the ground. "What the hell," she sniffed angrily. "Something grabbed my hand, and squeezed it." She stared at Daniel with a "bring it on" attitude.

"Oh shit," laughed Daniel as he began to walk away in protest.

"Oh, I suppose the pot did that too, did it, Brandon?" asked Patricia.   "No, but…" said Brandon reluctantly.

"But what?" insisted Patricia.

"But maybe you imagined it," said Daniel.

"And I guess I imagined this, did I?" Patricia held up her left hand, showing a deep, bloody gouge.

"Jesus!" said Tom. "Let me see that." Tom looked at her hand "Come on, I'll take you back inside and get this wrapped up, I, uh, you, uh, we, could do with a drink."

Daniel waited for them both to go back into the house. Then he turned to Brandon. "She cut it on something during the rush from the table, right?"

"Yep," said Brandon. "But I take no pleasure in saying so, so don't ask me to repeat it."

The Next Night—Babysitting

Jessica was reading the children a bedtime story when the phone rang. Jessica put the book down, walked to the landing, and picked up the phone. She stood with her back to the painting.

"Oh hi, Mrs. Leyden. Yeah, the kids are fine. OK, no, that's fine, see you then. I'm putting them to bed now. OK, bye."

Jessica hung up the phone and returned to the room. She knelt down between the children's single beds. "OK, it's time to sleep."

George was half asleep, but woke up as soon as Jessica threatened to leave. "Oh, Jessica, can't you read to us a little longer?"

Olivia strengthened his case. " Yeah, come on, Jessica, please?"

"No, I've read you the whole Pied Piper story tonight." Jessica got up. "It's sleep time, now turn around and go to sleep."

The children lamented but begrudgingly agreed. Olivia turned toward the wall, and Jessica kissed her on her temple. George continued to lie on his back. "George, turn around and go to sleep."

"I *am* going to sleep."

"OK, then turn around."

"Why do I have to turn around?" asked a confused George. Jessica giggled embarrassedly. "I don't know," she chuckled. "Just something my mother always says. I'll have to ask her."

She kissed George on the forehead. Before she left, she switched on a dim night-light, which partially lit the room.

"Jessica?"

"Yes, Olivia?"

"Can you give me Alice?"

Jessica picked up Olivia's doll, Alice, from on top of a toy guitar. Alice's feet accidentally struck an unpleasant minor chord. Jessica handed Alice to Olivia, who took her doll and cuddled into it.

Jessica made her way downstairs. She chose the center of the brown leather sofa so she'd have the best view of the movie, an R-rated horror picture. She began to arrange her orthodontic head piece, she placed small sponges on the forehead and chin pads to stop them from hurting too much. Then she hooked two elastic bands on two upper molars and stretched the elastic bands on either side of the curved aluminium bar that ran down the middle of her face. She placed four sucking sweets on the coffee table in front of the sofa, and one in her mouth.

Eyes wide, only the headset's metal bar dividing the television screen, she watched. *Wait until Margaret and Sally hear about this, oh, and of course Josh.* It was nothing less than a chore, but Jessica had to sit through it. It wasn't about watching an 'R' rated horror movie, it was all about *having watched* an 'R' rated horror movie, she knew that. She hated horror movies, especially scary ones, but payday was tomorrow, when they'll understand she's seen it, she couldn't wait.

A half hour passed, through the screams and splintered doors on the screen, she could hear a noise, a noise from within the room. She paused the movie, waited, and heard nothing. It became immensely irritating, as the precise moment she would un-pause, she could hear it again. Again she paused. Again, nothing. Play, there it was, a kind of itching, electronic sound. On screen, the college kid's engine couldn't start. Just as the zombies' hands burst through the glass, Jessica paused the movie, holding the button down firmly. Then she slammed the control on the sofa and folded her arms.

She waited. Sitting on her legs as all teenager girls do, she leaned over and picked up another candy from the coffee table. *Damn, only one left now after this one, I'd better only suck, mustn't bite, mustn't bite.*

She began to untwist the noisy wrapper. She placed the wrapper on the glass coffee table. This time her patience served her. She could clearly hear the sound. An electronic squeaking. It wasn't coming from the back of the room where the piano was. That corner of the room was always so dark you could hardly see the piano, a black grand. The sound was nearer than that.

Jessica got up and slowly walked toward the sporadic noise. Her left ear found it, it was on the bookshelf. "My God, Peter, it's only you."

Squashed between two books, there stood a constricted Peter the toy parrot, his small wings twitching. Jessica picked him up, and then she shrugged her shoulders and placed him back down on the shelf in front of the offending books. "There, there's some room, you OK now?"

She sucked the sweet "OK?" She clapped, a short crisp clap in hope of triggering him to repeat. "Hey, what's wrong with you?" She picked him up, he was still, and then he flapped his wings. Jessica instinctively turned him over, and saw the switch was set to off. Peter did, however, repeat a sound, but it was not the clap or Jessica's voice. It was the sound of screams, human screams.

Jessica dropped the toy parrot on the terracotta floor, and it landed flapping and twitching, this innocent messenger transmitting lost voices of utter despair. The screams of a thousand lost souls, their voices pleading, begging to be set free, a tortured chorus of the damned picked up on a frequency otherwise inaudible to a living ear. The parrot fluttered sporadically and gradually stopped. Like a dying animal, the screams became distant and faded. Jessica stared at it, the candy dropped it seemed in slow motion from her mouth and cracked on the floor into splinters of emerald sugar.

Jessica didn't dare pick Peter back up. She just walked backward to the sofa. Jessica knew nothing of electronics but she did recall hearing a police message come over the car radio once. *Dad said it was channel interference. I guess it happens, sometimes.*

She didn't un-pause. She wasn't going to watch the rest of the movie. She looked to her right over at the phone. *Just a quick call to the Leydens, just to see when they'll be back.* She reached over to the coffee table for her last candy, but the table was bare. A pulse of ice bolted through her veins and came to rest at the top of her head. She was certain she had one left, more than certain; she *did* have one more left. From the black corner of the room behind the piano, she heard the familiar crackling sound of plastic wrapper unsticking from a candy.

She asked a question, "George?" But she knew it wasn't him, she had only asked to console herself. To her right was the door, and it was open, to the right of that door, just a few steps along the hallway was the front door. She could run, run away. But she didn't. Jessica couldn't move. She could see the door, but it was not even an option for her, she was too scared to consider it.

I don't want to go to the door. I don't want to run. She tried to pacify something.

The candy was hurled from the dark black corner and exploded on the edge of the coffee table. Jessica flinched, but still did not move from the sofa. She stared toward the black corner of the room. She didn't blink. From behind that black piano, two shapes began to appear. These shapes did not seem to move, and yet they grew closer.

Jessica could hear the heavy thud of her heart. It seemed to dictate the very rate and rhythm of their approach. Jessica was screaming at the very top of her lungs; at least, that's what she thought. But those screams in reality emerged as tiny pathetic murmurs from her closed lips.

The two shadows emerged from the darkness and continued their advance. The boy looked blankly at Jessica, like a dog who doesn't understand a command. His eyes were completely black. He opened his mouth and raised his arms for an embrace. Jessica's screams began to blurt through her closed lips. He curled his small thin fingers, reaching for her, begging for her. The boy and the doll grew closer until they were at no more than arm's length from Jessica.

Jessica's voice managed to break through. She said, through trembling lips, "I won't run, I don't want to run."

She slowly commanded her arms up. The boy looked at her arms as they slowly lifted. He and the doll stopped. He looked at

Jessica, his mouth still gaping, but now gaping in surprise, in confusion. He dropped his arms violently to his sides and held them straight down, clenching his small white fists. He began to shake, and then he threw his head backward and forward, meeting Jessica's terrified eyes with his scream.

Jessica began to command her legs, but they did not obey. She rolled onto the floor and began to drag herself toward the door. She looked at him as she scrambled backwards. He was enraged, he was crying, shedding tears, but tears of blood. Jessica could not escape. The boy leaned over Jessica, he opened his mouth unnaturally wide, the inhuman sounds he expelled violated the very air. He grabbed Jessica's wrists, his sunken face inches from hers. He pulled her into him, his mouth opened wide, he tried to devour her, but her orthodontic head piece was in the way, keeping him inches from her face. With all of the strength Jessica could find, she programmed her leg, painstakingly executing each command, she placed her knee under her chest and pushed with her final bit of energy against that demonic body. Jessica felt hands behind her, pulling her up.

"Jessica, Jessica!" shouted Daniel.

Jessica continued kicking, unaware that it was Daniel. Daniel shouted her name again and again, and she finally stopped kicking. She turned around and stared at Daniel. Patricia ran into the room and held Jessica. Jessica could not speak.

"My God, what's happened, Jessica?" asked Patricia.

"You take care of her," Daniel said. "I'll check the kids."

A few intense moments later, Patricia had poured Jessica some water and sat her down on a dining room chair. Daniel joined them.

"The kids are sound asleep."

Jessica looked up from her glass. "I, I was watching a movie, and Peter started to scream, then my candies went missing, and one was being opened behind the piano. I thought it might be George, but somehow I knew it wasn't, then I saw…"

Jessica began to break down. Patricia leaned over and held her in a motherly embrace.

Jessica broke away. She stared at them both, astonished by what she herself was about to say. "It was the boy and that doll." She intentionally paused, and she wiped the tears from her face. Then, with defiance, she screamed:

"From the painting."

There was no attempt to respond, only a respectful silence. Daniel glanced over at the television screen, where he saw a paused spectacle of zombie hands bursting up through damp grass. He looked at Patricia, but she strongly resented his implication.

The New Hampshire Paranormal Society

The next day

Patricia's heart sank. She was peering out through a slit in the net curtains, and then it arrived. A black 1970's GMC van with round purple bubble windows on the side. Large green lettering read: "New Hampshire Paranormal Society." Damn" said Patricia. "'Discretion assured' my ass".

A young woman in flared maroon cords got out from the driver's side, the crisp winter sun making her squint as she looked around for the Leydens' house. A thin young man got out from the passenger's side and made his way to the back of the van. *Oh dear, that's Shaggy, if a Scooby gets out*... thought Patricia.

The doorbell rang. Patricia straightened her blouse and ran her hands over her face. She fixed her smile and then opened the door. The two ghost hunters stood there with an assortment of bags and two strong aluminium lock cases at their feet, like long-lost relatives come to stay.

"Hi," Urska said, beaming. Mateusz gave Patricia a child-like wave. Patricia opened the door wide and peered out to see if anyone was watching as Urska and Mateusz entered the hallway.

"Thanks for coming over on such short notice. Wow! You have lots of stuff," said Patricia.

"Yes," said Mateusz in a strong Polish accent. "We have many expensive equipments here."

*

Holding fresh cups of tea, they all stood looking at the painting.

"So, according to what you told us on the call, the previous owner said this child and doll, or whatever they are, were coming out of the painting?" said Urska.

"And he photographed this?" finished Mateusz.

Patricia gave them a controlled smile. "Well, yes, that's what the listing said, and he posted the photos. To me, it didn't look like much. It didn't look like he captured anything, and anyway, I don't really believe in such things."

Mateusz sipped his last drop of tea. "But you must believe a little, otherwise we wouldn't be here?" He smiled and looked at Urska.

"Well," said Patricia. "Like I said on our call this morning, I suppose it's the combination of events, the children I heard on the call with my friend, Olivia's painting, and the weirdness of the exploded pressure cooker. But it's what our babysitter said happened last night that convinced me to make the call to you."

"But you say your husband does not agree?" Urska said.

"No," said Patricia firmly. "He says it's nothing but coincidence and suggestive thinking."

Urska nodded. "That can sometimes be the case. I mean, you did know about the claims of it being supernatural, right?"

Patricia replied, "Yes, well, of course I did."

"And the babysitter?" asked Urska.

"No," said Patricia. "I kind of mentioned it, but not in any real detail. She's only a teenager, and as my husband was quick to point out, she was watching a horror movie when, you know, when she thought she saw something."

"Well, it could be that such a strong message played on her mind, and your mind of course. And even your little girl could have picked up something. Especially little ones, they are very open, no preconceptions are there to prevent or limit possibilities, it could easily explain why her drawing at school … I mean, it is a very strong image." Urska paused, then pointed at the signature on the bottom right-hand side of the painting: "W. Stoneham."

Patricia gestured for Mateusz's empty cup, which he handed to her with a grateful nod.

Urska wrote down the artist's name in a small blue reporter's note pad. "I'll explain what we're going to do, can we go somewhere more comfortable?" she said. Patricia smiled timidly in acknowledgment. Urska picked up a bag and she and Patricia began to make their way down to the dining room. Urska paused on the stairway and wretched. "Oh dear!" cried Patricia. "Are you OK?"

Urska grabbed her stomach. "Oh, how peculiar."

Mateusz bolted down beside her. "What's wrong?"

"Nothing, nothing," she wiped her watery eyes. "Nothing, it must have been the tea, I drank it too fast."

Patricia said, "Let me take your cup please?"

"No. no, I can take it down, your little tray is too full," she smiled and breathed in. "I feel OK now, wow."

Mateusz smiled as he caressed Urska's cheek. "You're OK, yeah?" Urska nodded. Mateusz stayed with the painting and started assembling an assortment of electronic gadgets.

Patricia placed the cups in the sink. "Allow me," said Urska as she gently placed her cup in the sink. "So, Mateusz will take photographs, many, many photographs. He will set up multiple readers, infrared, thermal, he will also leave sound recording equipment in certain spots around the house and near the painting."

Patricia looked worried, and Urska reassured her. "It's OK, all of this is just to see." Urska reached out and clasped Patricia's hands reassuringly. "I will tell you something, it is something that really should mean I can't do my job properly."

Patricia was intrigued, and Urska continued, beginning in a whisper, "I don't believe in ghosts."

This genuinely surprised Patricia. "Really?" she said.

Urska shook her head. "I won't tell Mateusz, ever, he believes, you see, he feels things, acutely. But in all my years doing this, I still have never seen anything absolutely credible, and I believe that makes me the perfect person to investigate these," she emphasized the word, 'occurrences.' "You see, someone who believes will see ghosts and demons in everything, and attribute every breeze and light flickering to a paranormal event. Not me. So be confident, whatever has happened here is probably just coincidence, just as your husband suggests. But at least we can rule out anything else, no?"

A comforted Patricia agreed. They made their way back upstairs to Mateusz, who was deep in concentration, looking down at a hand-held energy reader. He jumped when he noticed them both and quickly switched off the sensor and placed it back in a red duffle bag. He turned to Patricia with a smile. Urska knew this smile, he was nervous. "Do you have any oil? Like an olive oil, for example?"

Patricia responded, "Yes, I do, why?"

"Can you get it for me please? And three glasses of water?" Patricia was puzzled but didn't challenge the request and made her way back down the stairs.

Urska whispered to Mateusz, "The oil?"

Mateusz cleared off the small table under the painting; he placed the phone and note pad on the floor. He reached inside his duffle bag and took out the sensor. He switched it on, the sensor instantly went completely to the right, it red lined. He looked at Urska and raised his eyebrows. "Do you remember at the hotel, that stupidness about the chair? From that supposed rocking chair we picked up a two on this sensor and Cedric thought it was amazing." He looked back down at the sensor. "And here, it cannot go any further. Look, it goes to twenty, then there's a yellow strip then a red strip, then nothing just the manufacturers mark, we're literally off the scale here, even on the forums no one has ever reported a red-strip event, ever!" Urska's eyes were wide, and she didn't say a word.

Patricia placed a plastic tray on the small table. Mateusz handed Urska the bottle of oil, he pointed his finger over a glass filled about three-quarters full with water, Urska dribbled a few tiny drops of the oil over his finger. It dripped off his finger and into the water. After a few seconds, it settled on top of the water. He looked at Patricia and Urska.

"So what does that mean?" asked Patricia.

Mateusz responded, "It floats."

"Of course it floats, it's oil," said an unimpressed Patricia.

"Would you mind putting your finger over this glass?" said Mateusz courteously. She stuck her finger out over the second glass defiantly. Urska gently dribbled the oil over Patricia's finger. There had been no explanation of this ritual so far, and Patricia resented having to request one, nevertheless she began to feel dread at this simple performance. When the oil floated, it was only then that Mateusz smiled, with obvious relief. This reflected onto Urska, who also had to display her happiness with a smile as she exhaled.

Urska, still smiling, pointed her finger over the third glass as Mateusz delicately poured a tiny drop of oil on it. She said, "In Poland and many parts of Europe, they perform the oil test. As you said, Patricia, oil floats, right?"

Mateusz continued, "So the theory, or old wives' tale, as you call it, is that no one has an evil eye on you, or nothing is after you, if it floats."

Patricia relieved, giggled nervously. They all began to chuckle with the same relief. The chuckling began to slow, and then stopped. They were in complete silence. Urska's finger began to tremble as she stared into the glass.

"And this," said Mateusz, "means something *is* after you." The oil sat at the bottom of Urska's glass, not even a miniscule droplet remained on the surface. Instead, it sat mockingly the very bottom of the glass.

Urska controlled the tremble in her finger and wrestled her scared expression into a smile. "Huh, well I'm not Polish, I'm from Slovenia, so it doesn't count." Both she and Patricia laughed.

Mateusz obliged with a smile, but only because he didn't want to insist. Urska knew him too well, and she knew what this meant to him. His attempt to hide this from Urska only served to alarm her further. He decided to continue as casually as he could.

"So, I have placed some energy and audio sensors around and some camera triggers. If you see a flash in the night, don't jump up screaming 'ghost,' it could be many things."

"What about other areas of the house?"

"I will place some downstairs, in some rooms, and basement rooms and garage, and also in the room with the piano." Mateusz deliberated over a question. "May I ask you something?"

"Sure," said Patricia.

"Why don't you get rid of it?"

Patricia shrugged apologetically. "Because I think I'm being silly." She punctuated this with a chuckle, just to make sure he understood it was just all silly. Mateusz didn't buy it.

"You think that?" Mateusz pointed at her. "*You?*"

Patricia looked down at her feet. After a few pensive moments, she raised her head back up, taking a deep, strengthening breath in through her nostrils, and she replied clearly, "No, no I don't, I don't believe I'm being silly at all."

Urska rubbed Patricia on the shoulder. "Remember what I said, that these events are almost always explained, even Mateusz will tell you, Mateusz tell her."

Urska placed her hand out flat beckoning Mateusz to deliver a supportive comment, instead he said, "Yes … *almost* always."

Patricia looked nervously at Urska. Urska could only return an embarrassed smile, as anything else was beyond her control. What Mateusz's quick comment had in cleverness it lacked in sensitivity, and consequently it inflicted damage. Patricia folded her arms and gently bit her bottom lip.

Paranormal Argument

Mateusz sat on the end of his bed, flicking through digital pictures from the Leyden visit.

"I didn't exaggerate," Mateusz said, angrily clicking the delicate camera buttons. "It *is* bad, the oil is *not* nonsense."

Urska pulled her cotton top off in equal rage. "Ah, but we were there to help her, and you just frightened her."

"No, no I didn't frighten her, I think you're angry because I frightened *you*."

Urska placed her knuckles on her hips in an aggressive stance. Her pink bra embroidered with delicate flowers looked so serene in comparison. "Me, scared? Are you crazy?"

"Yeah, yeah, I know you don't think much of all of this. Anyway, whatever." Mateusz continued to click without really looking at the photos.

"No, not really," Urska unzipped her trousers and let them fall to the floor. She stepped out of them, kicking them in the direction of a chest. They missed and landed comically on a lamp, mocking her anger, looking somewhat like a girl washing her long purple hair in a basin. Urska growled at them. "But it doesn't stop me from doing my job properly, and…"

"Urska!" Mateusz stopped his ferocious clicking and stared at Urska.

"What?" She snapped.

"Your legs."

Urska looked down at her naked legs. Tiny scratches ran up the front and backs of her calves. Urska screamed and jumped as if she had seen a mouse.

"Look!" said Mateusz. "Look at that! Explain that to me?"

Urska ran her hands over the scratches, and then she placed her hand on her stomach, and turned white and clammy, like an old oyster. "Oh, I feel sick again."

She ran to the bathroom and buckled down on her knees in front of the toilet. Mateusz followed her and gathered her long hair from in front of her face and held it behind her head. Urska began to wretch, but nothing came up. With each wretch, she curled up her back like an alley cat in a fight, but each time nothing came.

"Come on, we need to get you to a doctor," said Mateusz.

Urska sat down on the floor, panting. "It's OK, I feel a bit better now."

"But you didn't get sick, how can you feel better?"

She grabbed his hand. "Thanks, baby," she smiled.

Mateusz smiled back. "Baby? You never call me that … I like it though."

He kneeled down beside her and wrapped his arms around her. "Urska?"

"Yes?"

"We need to see Agnieska."

Urska pushed Mateusz. "What?"

Mateusz took a deep breath, he knew he'd need it. "Urska, the scratches, you're feeling sick, the oil, and a red stripe event. Please?"

"But you said yourself Agnieska is dangerous."

"I said you should never go to her unless you need to." He caressed her hair. "And we need to."

Urska looked down at her legs. "Maybe I scratched them on some bushes."

"When?" said Mateusz. "When was the last time you had bare legs? In September, I think. And look at the scratches, they run vertically down your legs."

"There's got to be an explanation," insisted Urska.

"Maybe, but let's speak to Agnieska, just to be sure."

"Agnieska!"

"Yes, Agnieska!" insisted Mateusz.

Urska paused and then conceded. "When?"

"Now."

Urska shouted, "No!" She placed her palms by the sides of her head. "No, there's got to be an explanation."

"What explanation can there be?"

"There can be hundreds of explanations," Urska snapped. After a few moments he went quiet and Mateusz didn't respond. She began to caress his hair. "Look, let me have a few days, if I don't feel better we will go to her, OK?"

Manuela's Afternoon

The next day

Manuela walked past the painting. She paused and stuck her tongue out at it. Clutching a white rosary chain, she blessed herself. She heard the cats crying to each other again. The same cold fingers worked their way around her stomach, and up her back, tingling up to the very tip of her head.

"You blasted cats, how much I hate you," she looked down the stairs at the general direction of this appalling conversation. "Hate you bastards."

Determinedly she walked downstairs and into the kitchen. She filled a basin with water, carried it to the front door, and opened the door by balancing the basin on one knee, but there were no cats. Yet the crying continued. She realized the crying came from within the house. Manuela continued her search, ignoring the cold heavy pit in her stomach.

"I hate you. You want to upset Manuela, hey? So you got inside, never mind, I will bathe you in water, bastards."

She followed the crying to the basement. She carefully walked down five wooden steps. As she passed each step, her inner voice told her not to proceed, but no one told Manuela what to do, especially weaklings.

"In the laundry, hey? Sleeping on my clean sheets, hey? I will stop your horrible crying, you should all be castrated."

The crying was very loud, *too loud*, thought Manuela, but she ignored such logic. She paused at the laundry door and listened to the guttural wailing. She was hesitant about entering the room, as the crying now sounded almost human. She switched on the fluorescent lights with her chin. Finally, after a deep breath, she kicked open the door. Her hands opened, she dropped the basin, there were no cats.

But there was something, something that was in fact almost human. Standing at the back of the laundry room, under the black and ice-blue of the flickering fluorescent light, was a small boy. The boy from the painting.

He was standing with his eyes and mouth wide open, his arms outstretched, beckoning to Manuela. He was crying, shedding tears of blood from his completely black eyes. The bloody tears streamed down his gaunt, pale face. His cries were not at her, but *for* her, he wanted her, he wanted her embrace; a mother's embrace, a mother's love. The doll appeared from behind him. They began to walk toward her, the strobe effect of the lights sending these spectres into darkness, then light. They moved with an unnatural plodding gait, edging their way forward, transported in the sharp leaps of blackness and light, and with every ice-blue flicker, they got nearer and nearer to Manuela. On top of their crying she heard herself screaming. This broke her from her frozen terror like a pinch from a dream. She was beyond panic, she was in an abyss; the only presence was absence, an absence of everything human.

Manuela tried to step backward, but her urgent brain signals were ignored by her muscles as her primary motor functions were overwhelmed, until they abandoned her completely. She collapsed back on to the step, physically paralyzed. The boy continued to beckon for his unwanted embrace. When he was almost upon her, his appearance began to change. His face grew sunken, and his expression conveyed ultimate agony. His small arms were still outstretched to Manuela, his thin fingers curled toward him, gesturing for her to come to him. Manuela was suspended between life and death, no longer feeling moored to her body, almost as if her soul was attempting to escape the intolerable horror from which her physical body was unable to remove itself. She succeeded, and the life slowly faded from her eyes.

I Am Trying, Detective Gomez

Gomez was pacing up and down, looking incredulously at Apsland. Apsland was sitting at his dining table, holding an item of clothing from one of the victims, a T-shirt. His eyes were closed. "I can feel her torment. Alone, lost, she tried to wake up, like a bad dream, she was willing herself to wake up. She realized it wasn't a dream, she is screaming, she is screaming."

Gomez threw his hands up in the air. "So she's screaming, I get it, she died a horrible death, we *know* that! Look at her, for Christ's sake."

Gomez put his finger on the crime scene photo and flicked it across the table at Apsland. Mutilated, the deadly realization captured upon her face.   Apsland jumped up from his chair. He leaned across the table.

"Detective Gomez, I am trying."

"I know you are, and I do appreciate it, but we're getting nowhere, nowhere. We've been cooped up here for over a week, and nothing."

Apsland slowly sat back down in his chair.

Gomez spun a chair around and sat down, resting his arms on its back. "There's nothing!" Gomez scooped up a dozen crime scene photographs and fanned them out in his hand. "Nothing." he turned them toward Apsland. "No wonder Manfreddi gave up, this killer doesn't go by age, sex, creed, religion, no house owner has ever had any connection to the next victim, bearing in mind the ones that go missing eventually get killed too. So what is it about? Yeah, I see he has an M.O., eyes out and mutilation, but there's no pattern in his choice of victims."

"Can you stop saying 'he'?" asked Apsland. "I think it could mislead us."

"It's just for speed. I'll say 'they' from now on, OK?"

"Can we use 'it' instead?" Apsland inquired.

Gomez smirked. "Sure, why not?"

"I'm no criminal physiologist, detective," said Apsland. "But I don't think it needs a pattern."

"I know. It'd sure help, though," quipped Gomez.

Agnieska

Agnieska lived about twenty miles away in a small, semi-abandoned industrial town. Mateusz didn't say much en route, though if he had said something, it would have been "I told you so." Urska just leaned her head against the window. Mateusz switched the radio on to drown out their thoughts. Urska's stomach was still churning; she had not eaten for three days and had lost a considerable amount of weight. Mateusz's stomach was also churning, but this was brought on by anxiety. He knew something was wrong, something bad. Otherwise he would never go to Agnieska. Talking to Agnieska was like walking through an ancient labyrinth, touch the wrong wall and your fate is sealed.

He felt like Perseus on his way to the Medusa.

He only knew this by her reputation, he had never actually been to see her before.

Now, sitting in this silly room, it was predictably similar to how he imagined it would be. She had converted her basement into a type of chamber. The walls were draped in red velvet, a tacky red chandelier hung from a dirty ceiling. Mateusz couldn't help thinking it looked like an old whorehouse. Just as he thought that, he noticed an old ad for condoms partially hidden behind a collection of jigsaw puzzles. *What the hell?* he thought *maybe it was.* Urska sat at a table covered with a green cloth, looking as pious and delicate as if she were waiting to see the pope.

An ugly man with no chin and stinking of vinegar came into the room. Mateusz handed him some money. Urska tried to see the amount; it looked around a hundred dollars. The man disappeared behind a curtain and Agnieska immediately appeared. Mateusz remained standing. Urska continued to look at the table, out of respect, or maybe fear.

Mateusz began to speak to Agnieska in Polish. Urska couldn't understand anything, but she read his gestures. Mateusz touched his legs and then his stomach. After what seemed too many words, he extended his finger. *That's the oil*, thought Urska. Agnieska took a seat facing Urska, and Mateusz remained standing. Agnieska only said the occasional "*Tak*" in a low voice. Mateusz showed Agnieska the photographs.

Agnieska looked at Mateusz and then at Urska. She clapped her hands; the ugly man appeared from the curtain, and she mumbled something to him in Polish. The ugly man handed Mateusz back his money and returned back behind the curtain.

"*Czemu*?" asked Mateusz.

Agnieska explained to Mateusz that she returned the money because she could do nothing, and that Urska had been cursed. To which Mateusz explained that he knew she had been cursed, and that was why he was there. He was careful not to sound rude in any way, as he didn't want to offend Agnieska. They had enough problems.

A loose English translation of their conversation went something like this:

Agnieska: "She will die."

Mateusz: "Can you not do anything?"

Agnieska: "No, I told you already, I cannot do anything."

Mateusz: "There must be something?"

Agnieska: "No, nothing."

Mateusz: "Then I will destroy the painting, I will burn it."

Agnieska: "That will not work, it will not undo what is done."

Urska couldn't understand the words, but she understood the intent, words were not necessary. Mateusz ran to Urska and knelt by her. Agnieska looked fiercely at Urska and then pointed at Mateusz. *"Kto z nią zostanie ten zginie."*

Mateusz stood up and walked behind Urska. He turned and shouted back at Agnieska in Polish, he didn't care any longer what buttons he pressed. Urska knew Mateusz wouldn't speak to Agnieska like that unless he had nothing to lose.

Urska stood up and shouted at Agnieska, "Tell me, tell me what you said!"

Mateusz screamed. "No, please, please don't tell her!"

Agnieska calmly spoke in broken English. "You will die, and whoever with you will die too, this boy say he stay with you."

Urska trembled. "Well, I don't believe it." Urska grabbed the green tablecloth and yanked it across the table, overturning a brass candle stick. She turned and ran out of the room, barging past Mateusz.

Mateusz quickly followed her. They both ran up into the welcome sunlight. But the distant winter rays could not warm them. Urska had her back to him, and he spun her around. She was slightly annoyed at him for doing this, as she hadn't finished wiping away the evidence of her tears.

"Well, that went well, didn't it?" she said in a fragile voice.

Mateusz gently tilted up her chin with the side of a finger. "I don't care what that silly hag says."

"I was thinking, why don't we just burn it?" asked Urska desperately.

Mateusz threw his head back in pain and squeezed his eyes shut. "She says that won't work."

Urska smiled sadly. "But do you believe what she said?"

"No, no," said Mateusz. He made sure each "no" was perfect, a proper believable "no," a "no" with integrity. He was so successful that it went some way toward actually convincing himself that the old hag might in fact be wrong.

"But tomorrow I will go to the Leydens and take back the equipment, just in case. That way, if there is some malvelot thing, then we can wipe it away from us."

"Malevolent" giggled Urska as she corrected his pronunciation.

"OK, true," smiled Mateusz. "Malvelot?" he smiled even more strongly. "OK? Malvelot?"

Urska chuckled, "OK, perfect."

Urska's Morning

Urska awoke in an empty bed. The beauty of awaking from the suspended reality of a dream is that everything is reset. It's a Zen moment when you don't have good or bad thoughts. It only lasts for a second or two, but the seconds pass and the world hits you, your world. If you're in a good space, then that second can pass into your real World quickly, and you don't care. Urska did care, her second passed, and she braced herself against the bed as if it were a fairground Gravitron. She felt a diabolical sense of dread. She had intended to annihilate the demons before getting out of bed, through logic and reason, but the pain in her stomach told her there were other plans in store.

Nevertheless, she sat upright in bed and pushed her shoulders back, clicking her sternum and assuming a confident posture. She looked like a boxer, you could almost see a man standing behind her, rubbing her shoulders and miming a left jab, and another with a towel on his forearms, rubbing Vaseline under her eyes.

She felt like Wile E. Coyote; like she had run off the edge of a cliff and yet was still running. *That's OK*, she thought. *As long as I don't look down, I won't fall, it works for him.*

She got up and ran to the bathroom as fast as she could. Back on the floor again. She resented getting so familiar with that part of the bathroom; the different tubes that worked their way behind the toilet and the uncomfortable vicinity of the toilet brush to her face.

She heaved. Nothing. She sat back on her legs. "Fuuuck," she said, and she didn't normally swear. *Here comes another train.* Heave. Nothing. All fine, maybe it will pass, the world might be OK after all, there's still hope, isn't there? *Aahh shit, is that another train*? Heave. She squeezed her eyes shut. Whatever was in her stomach raced up her throat and splattered into the bowl. She felt instantly better. She reached around to her left and unrolled some toilet paper to dry her eyes and mouth.

She looked down into the bowl. She jumped backwards and hit the back of her head on the door. *That's not real, that can't be real.* She slowly made her way back to the bowl and stared in. Staring back at her, literally, were six or seven eyes. It was hard to count all of them correctly, as some floated on top of others.

You will die and whoever is with you will die too.

Urska never liked the casual use of important words, particularly sentimental words. She'd struggled with that when she first came to America, where everyone "loved" each other. For her, she thought the words had lost their power. Her favourite expressions were: "Talk is cheap" and "Actions speak louder than words." Mateusz once told her he loved her, and she once told him. Only once, and she always felt she had gone against her own principles in telling him that, as she wasn't really sure.

She was sure now. Why? Because she wasn't crying, she was busy packing her bags like a Navy SEAL on a mission. She knew she loved him, just as she knew she would never see him again.

*

The first thing Mateusz noticed when Patricia opened the door was that she was wearing black. He could see Daniel in the background, adjusting a black tie.

"Who's that?" said Daniel.

"It's the investigator," she shouted to Daniel, who shook his head. "What are you doing here?" she asked Mateusz.

"There has been a death?" inquired Mateusz. "Yes, our housekeeper, Manuela."

"I need to get my things." Mateusz was nervous. "Can I come in? I need to get my things."

Patricia was instantly concerned. "Why?"

She held the door open and Mateusz entered, saying, "I've just gotten a job opportunity in Phoenix and I must leave immediately."

They walked up the stairs, out of Daniel's earshot.

Patricia stopped him just before they reached the landing. "That's bull," she whispered forcefully.

Mateusz pointed behind her. "My things, please. How did she die?"

"What's wrong?" Patricia insisted.

Mateusz politely but determinedly swerved past her, rubbing his body painfully against the banisters. He began to collect all of his equipment and threw it in a bag. Patricia noted his casual treatment of the expensive items.

"How's Urska?"

Mateusz ignored her.

"How's Urska?" said Patricia in a raised voice.

"She's fine," said Mateusz, looking at the floor, avoiding eye contact with Patricia and the painting. "Please forgive us."

"No, I don't forgive you," said Patricia. "You have a job here, you can't just go."

Mateusz turned to Patricia. "I wasn't asking *you* for forgiveness."

"What's going on up there?" asked Daniel.

Mateusz threw his bag over his shoulder and ran down the stairs to the living room. He bent down under the piano and picked up another sensor. Patricia was following closely behind him.

"Mateusz?" she asked.

He rushed into the hallway and picked up another gadget from beside a hat stand. He put his hand on the front door knob, and then he turned and looked at Patricia. He hesitated, he was about to say something, but he changed his mind. He opened the door and ran outside.

Patricia ran up to the door. She folded her arms and stamped her foot. "Damn it!"

Mateusz spun his van around so hard he left a semi-circular donut mark on the street.

"Something I said?" smirked Daniel.

"Holy shit," said Patricia.

"What?"

"I wanted them here, do you understand that? And now Manuela's dead. I wanted them here."

"Yeah, well, I didn't. And again, Manuela had a heart attack, the coroner confirmed it. And by the way, last night I got a nude picture of me taken before and after going to the toilet, so one from the front and one from the back," Daniel sneered. "Furthermore, those outfits record all of our conversations. Those sensors don't just pick up ghouls, in fact they don't pick up ghouls, cos ghouls don't exist, but they do pick up Brandon talking to me about tax havens, the Cayman Islands E-T-C, E-T-C. Those conversations do exist, and for all you know, this is just a scam to get information."

Patricia didn't bite back. Strangely, she welcomed Daniel's absurd argument. *Maybe if I join him in his bubble, nothing more will happen.*

"Maybe you're right, honey," Patricia said as she walked past him.

Daniel had already taken a breath to begin the next compelling instalment of his argument, but once her words registered he was disarmed; the energy from his inhalation consequently aborted like a phantom sneeze.

Funeral

"Hi," said Urska.

"Hello," said Daniel, "what can I do for you?"

"Um. I am Urska, is Mrs. Leyden here, please?"

"No, she's dropping our children off at school. Can I help you?"

"I am from the paranormal investigation team."

Daniel's expression relaxed.

"Can I come in for a moment?" asked Urska.

Daniel shrugged his shoulders. "Sure." Urska entered the hallway; she was shivering.

"Are you OK?" inquired Daniel. "Can I make you some tea? You look like you could do with some warming up."

"No," said Urska, with a smile. "I'm fine, thanks."

"What can I do for you? You know your co-worker was here not long ago?"

"Yes, yes, I know, Mateusz. He came for his equipment," Urska said, nodding.

"Yes, and then he ran out of here like a madman," said Daniel.

He remembered something, and held up his finger. "Hold on…"

Daniel walked into the dining room and came back swiftly with something in his hand. "Please give this to, to … uh…"

"Mateusz," said Urska.

"Yes," said Daniel. "He forgot it, it was down in the laundry room. I don't know what it is, but … well, anyway, please take it to him."

"It's a night-vision camera," said Urska glumly. "Anyway, it's for a simple reason I am here, I needed to investigate the painting, your painting, but I realized I left my notebook at home and I had written the name of the artist in it, and I was in the area, so I thought…"

"I understand," smiled Daniel. "It's a W. Stoneham."

"Ah, that's right."

Daniel smiled again. An awkward silence fell. Daniel shrugged and asked, "Anything else?"

"No, no thanks," said Urska, but her manner was timid.

"Are you sure?" Daniel asked, in an encouraging tone.

"Well, there is something, but I was hoping to speak to Mrs. Leyden."

"I'm afraid that'll be difficult today. As soon as she's back we both need to go out, we have to go to a funeral."

"A funeral?" asked Urska. "Whose?"

Daniel responded reluctantly, wishing he hadn't mentioned it at all. "Our housekeeper."

"How did she die?"

"Please let's not," Daniel said impatiently. "She had a heart attack, it's simple."

"You're *both* going out?" inquired Urska.

"Yes, so you may as well tell *me* what you had to tell her. I can pass it along, I don't bite," advised Daniel with an encouraging nod.

"No, maybe I shouldn't. Mrs. Leyden said you don't believe in any of this," said Urska sadly.

"She's right," said Daniel. "I find the whole thing ludicrous. I love the story, that's why I bought the painting in the first place. Yeah, sure, a few things have happened, but that's only because we conditioned our minds to the story. So it says it's haunted on eBay, and the owner saying the kids left the painting and…"

Urska cupped her face with her hands.

"What's wrong?" asked a concerned Daniel.

"You must get rid of that painting," said Urska, her voice muffled through her hands.

"Listen, please, this is all just a story. You mustn't get carried away. I know it's your field of work, but you'll upset yourself for nothing."

"You must get rid of that painting," Urska repeated, only this time she growled.

"Look, don't worry about the painting. The painting is my problem," said Daniel.

"No, it's my problem too," said Urska. She slowly bent over and pulled up her pant legs, revealing the scratch marks. "Please, just tell your wife."

"Are those scratches?" Daniel asked.

"Yes," replied Urska. "Little scratches, from little hands."

*

Mateusz arrived back home. He was about to shout Urska's name but instead ran straight up the stairs to the bedroom, three steps at a time. He stared at the empty bed, and the note left upon it.

After a few seconds, he snatched it.

"I still felt sick this morning so I have gone to the doctor, I'll be back around eleven XX"

Mateusz folded the note into a tiny square as he stared ahead blankly. He looked at his watch. It was just past 9:15. He made his way downstairs and began to prepare some coffee. *I don't know her doctor.* He screwed the cap on his Italian coffee maker and placed it on a burner. *Maybe she really does have just a bad stomach.*

He turned on the gas and leaned over the coffee pot. He ran over the facts one by one, they were all in order. So why did he feel like he was looking for his hat while wearing his hat? The coffee began to burble up through the filter spout, it bubbled away until all of the coffee had pushed through, and then it began to calm, just a few lingering pops. Mateusz switched off the stove automatically. He looked down the hall and then looked up to the ceiling. In an instant, he bolted toward the stairs and leaped up them like an expert in Parkour. He stood in front of their closet and opened it. Her backpack was gone, but her clothes all seemed to be there. He opened the drawers—her underwear, tights and socks were missing. He ran to the bathroom; her toothbrush was gone.

*

At last Urska could feel the vibration of the garage door opening from where she leaned against the wall. The Leydens' car rolled down the driveway. Urska pushed herself against the wall as flat and as invisible as she could make herself. The car stopped. *Come on, come on go, just go. Go before the door goes down.*

The door began to close. *Damn!* But finally they started to drive off. Urska took her chance and swept into the garage and immediately snuck into a corner.

The door closed, and the bright horizontal line of winter sunshine disappeared at the top of the garage door, leaving Urska in complete blackness. But she had memorized the way to the door before the garage door had shut. She was halfway or thereabouts to the inner door. The Leydens had an extra spin dryer for sheets; there wasn't enough space in laundry room so they installed it in the garage. It came on full blast but Urska instantly realized what it was, so the sound didn't scare her, or even make her jump. What she also realized though, and what *did* scare her, was that now she couldn't hear anything but this loud noise, all at once she was blind *and* deaf.

Urska waved her arms in front of her. She could feel she was almost at the door. Her hand brushed over something, she waved her hand back around the area but there was nothing. *How can that be? If it was an object, why is it not there anymore?* She pushed her dread into a holding area and recommenced waving her arms. At last she found the door. She lifted the metal latch and opened the door, it fell open with a thud. She bolted out as if jumping over lava and immediately slammed it shut again, trying to stamp out her chills with some small shrieks. She ran up the small set of stairs to the Leydens' hallway. Only then did she turn around and look back at the closed door. She also took a peek at the dread that she had managed to park in the holding area. *What was that?*

Urska made her way up the stairs until she was in front of the painting. She took off her backpack and reached into a side pocket. Immediately she put her backpack back on. She needed to do this and get out.

She held up her lighter to the middle of the painting, and then moved it over and down to the bottom right-hand corner. Then she flicked open the chrome top.

She heard a noise. There was no question of what it was. It was the small metal latch on the internal garage door. Clink, and drop, clink and drop. Whatever was trying couldn't quite open it. She refocused and flicked at the striker with her thumb, but got only sparks. Urska trembled, again she could hear the clink, and drop. She tried again. Sparks.

"No, please," she begged. Clink, and drop.

Urska looked down the stairs. She looked back at her lighter, she struck it again with her thumb, and this time it lit, a long steady flame. Urska held it against the painting.

And then a thud: the internal garage door was opened. A sharp gust of air blew out the flame on Urska's lighter.

The pitter-patter of little feet, demon feet, raced up from the basement. The violence in the footsteps told Urska to run, she didn't want to see what it was. She ran into the Leydens' bedroom and slammed the door; to her relief, there was a key, but her trembling hand and panicked mind could not lock the door, she was turning the key clockwise. Tiny, yet heavy footsteps ran right up to the door. Then silence. She looked down at the doorknob. It slowly began to turn.

"Go away!" she pleaded. "Go away!" She managed to salvage a moment of lucid thought; she turned the key counter-clockwise and locked the door.

There was silence, then a great thud, and another, and another, until the door was being shaken violently. Urska pushed with all of her might against the door and held the door-knob as firmly as she could.

Urska continued to scream "Go away!" at the invading force.

"Urska! Let me in."

"Mateusz?"

"Yes, let me in."

"My God, Mateusz!" She scrambled to unlock the door, but again turned the key counter-clockwise.

"Let me in."

"Hold on," Urska fumbled. "Hold on."

"Let me in! Let me in! Let me in! Let me in!"

The door began to shudder violently. Urska stopped what she was doing. She walked backward, shaking her head, and she began to scream in short identical bursts one after the other. The voice at the door was now unrecognizable, and each request to be let in was followed by laughter. Urska covered her ears. She turned to the window. She unbolted it and opened it. Alarms instantly went off. She threw herself out, not considering or caring in the slightest as to where or how she would land.

She scrambled up from the grass and fled into the middle of the street. She looked up at the house. The alarms shrieked as they flashed their ice-blue beacons, and the laughter, that laughter. She turned and began to run, the sounds of the house getting fainter and fainter. The last to fade was the laughter; it was so completely invasive that Urska's mind could still hear it in her head, cackling away. Even later, as she stared out of the bus window into the busy streets, she could hear it.

*

Twelve people looked into a pit, gathered around like a horseshoe. It was either their collective body heat that was responsible for the gap in the fog, or the physical wall they created. It only assisted to clear the view in front of them, however, the center of the horseshoe; it had no effect upon the undulating shapes that stood behind them.

That cold blanket penetrated identically and deeply without prejudice; be it crooked headstones, naked trees, or bones, those above ground or those below.

The horseshoe lost its shape as the parties disappeared into the blanket back to their vehicles. Leaving Manuela's husband surrounded on either side by two tall columns of his own flesh and blood, Manuel and Pablo.

Daniel shook Manuela's husband's hand. "She meant a great deal to us all, the whole family will miss her."

"Thank you. You know, she was as strong as an ox. She never said nothing about no heart problem. You know, even the doctor said she was in good health. Then this, a big heart attack and, and gone."

Patricia's vocal cords were closed like a gate on a dam. The words "I'm so sorry" opened the gate, and were washed away before they were complete. Manuela's husband smiled at Patricia and embraced her. By consoling her, he consoled himself.

"Today, before the funeral, I was alone with her. I touched her arm, it was cold, her arms were always cold. 'Don't touch my arms,' she used to say, she hated me touching her arms, because they were fat. But I used to cool my cheek on them in the summer, and I think secretly she liked it. But today, they were the same, not colder than normal, so I felt she could even be alive. I rested my cheek there one more time."

*

Daniel and Patricia began their long drive home. It was raining heavily. Patricia's flood had finally relieved, however she knew better than to shut the gate just yet.

Patricia wiped her nose. Her voice was an octave lower from the crying.

"You know, the thing I can't forget is her expression." She leaned her head back on the headrest and shut her watery eyes tightly, squeezing a tear from either side. "I'm just so glad the kids didn't find her."

Daniel avoided continuing the conversation. "Let's just get home. What time is it?"

Patricia looked at her phone.

"Six-thirty. We're about two hours from home, I'll call Cynthia and see how the kids are doing." Then she huffed, a huff that was a precursor to a lengthy debate.

Daniel understood. "I don't want to talk about it," he said as he stared at the road.

"Well, I do," said Patricia.

"I've said it time and time again, it's just coincidence. The phone, a crossed line; the painting by Olivia, just a weird fluke; Manuela, a hundred pounds overweight and too many tacos; and Jessica! She made all that up, just something to tell her friends at school." He punctuated every "explanation" with a raised tone and a shrug of his shoulders, like he was telling her facts: 'the thigh bone's connected to the knee bone, the knee bone's connected to the leg bone' and so on. He was only convincing himself. He continued, however, because he was enjoying himself. "And your hand, you cut that on something when the pressure cooker exploded. When the pain finally hit, you thought it was someone holding your hand but it was just the pain beginning to register in your hand." He turned and stared at her.

Patricia just pointed ahead. "Look at the road."

A few moments of silence passed. Daniel cracked his neck like boxers do for some reason. Patricia took this as some kind of subconscious victory ritual. She assumed he must have taken her lack of response as confirmation of her agreement.

"What about what happened to you?" she asked.

"Me? What happened to me?"

"The first night we hung the painting. You thought the kids were there in the bedroom, didn't you?"

"Ah, now," he pointed his finger in the air. "All I did was dream the kids were in the room."

"But they weren't, were they?" said Patricia.

"No! That's why I said it was a dream."

*

Urska sat at the table. The diner was cast in a perpetual shadow underneath a train track, sapping the color from anything visible through the rain-drenched stencilled windows 'all day breakfast' mirror image painted on the glass. The rattling of the train as it passed sounded like Jack's giant waking up at the top of the beanstalk.

Ketchup in a plastic tomato-shaped container, all caked up around the spout. Salt, pepper and toothpicks. There was also a small steel tub for sugar, the white sugar, spotted with asteroid shaped sugar balls of differing tones of brown.

A waitress kept staring at her but wouldn't come over. Urska smiled, or tried to. She lifted her hand from the sticky table and gave a discreet wave for service.

The waitress walked over to a man serving behind the counter, and they talked in whispers. Urska was baffled, wondering what was so interesting. *They can't read my mind so what do they know?* Finally, the waitress arrived, her apron busy keeping her gut in. Urska noticed she had a pencil behind each ear. *Each ear! Maybe she's ambidextrous and can take two orders at the same time. No, no, she can't, she's just stupid and hasn't realized.*

"Yep, what'll it be?"

"I'd like a coffee, please."

"Anything else?"

"No thank you, I'm not too hungry."

"Nah, I didn't think so, you people never eat."

"You people?"

The waitress looked at the man behind the counter, and then back at Urska.

"Nothing," said the waitress into her notepad.

"No, you tell me what you mean by 'you people'?"

The man from behind the counter leaned over on his thick hairy elbows and in a broad, ugly accent said, "Junkies, she means junkies." As befit his broad, ugly accent, he was a broad, ugly man, with frizzy hair that almost looked pubic, and a nose shaped like a cauliflower.

Urska was disarmed; the shock had done that. She thought maybe they didn't like her accent, maybe they don't like immigrants, but junkie? She became aware of the diners staring at her; they were staring at her with what could only be sympathy. There was an old, dishevelled black man wearing more layers than an onion. An old lady pasted in the same makeup that had once upon a time worked for her, once upon a long time before this day, there she was now dining at Mario's, gumming away at her ham and eggs. Ah, Daisy! If the old gang could see her now, but they can't, they're all dead.

"I'm not a junkie," said Urska. "How dare you!"

"OK, honey, sure," said Mario. The real Mario, Mario the First, was long dead of a heart attack. In fact, this latest Mario, Mario III, had never even met Mario the First; but he had met Savas, who was Mario II, and Savas had met Mario the First. Mario III told his wife (the waitress) on more than one occasion, 'It's just like the James Bond actors, it's the same thing, all playing the role one after the other.' Mario III doesn't think it's funny. His wife does, but she doesn't tell him that, she just despises him instead.

He nodded to his wife, who motioned the glass coffee pot in the direction of Urska's cup.

Urska stood up straight like an Irish dancer. "What? Are you crazy?" she picked up her backpack from the plastic seat beside her. "I'm not staying here to be insulted."

Urska stormed out, and she made sure she stormed. *They got the message, degenerates.*

Mario III turned to his wife as she pulled her apron corset in even tighter.

"You know what I should'a said?"

"No, whut?" she said, her hands busy behind her back, wrestling with the apron strings.

"I should'a said 'Yeah, there are plenty o' places you can go to be insulted lady'."

"Yeah, that would have been funny if you had said that, why don't you run after her and tell her? She's probably only a block or two away."

He pointed at Daisy with his short stubby pinkie. "Give Daisy a refill." He smiled at Daisy. "You think I'm funny, don't yah, honey?"

Daisy licked the egg off her chin; she heard none of it.

*

Shitty hole, shitty people. Urska's storming out and her anger helped delay the assault on her dignity. It wore off though, she knew it would, and when it did, Urska began to cry. She convinced herself it was because she needed Mateusz and missed him, and she did, but she didn't need those shits at the diner, especially now, didn't she have enough on her plate? *For Christ's sake?* She looked up at the sky. *Why am I looking up at the sky? God knows!* She shook her head. *No, no he doesn't, he doesn't know why I'm crying, he doesn't know why I am to die,* "and he doesn't even know why I am looking up!" she screamed.

She took out a tissue and began to wipe her tears. She looked back up to the sky, her eyes blinking away rain. She screamed, "I'm looking up for you, for *you*, you cruel, useless fucking bastard!" She collapsed next to a derelict bronze two-door saloon car, she looked up at the chrome mirror and twisted it into view. A face she barely recognised stared back.

She means junkie, junkie, junkie, junkie.

Urska closed her eyes. A shadow passed over her closed eyes and the rain stopped its unrelenting tap-dance on her thin face.

"Excuse me, miss?"

Urska opened her eyes. A young policeman was peering down at her; he held an umbrella.

"Are you OK?" he inquired genuinely.

Urska suddenly felt valued. His sincerity had obliterated any second-guessing as to his motives.

"Not so good," Urska said with a sad smile.

"Here, let me help you up."

He grabbed her thin elbow and pulled her to her feet. He brushed her shoulders down with his free hand, interjecting a comforting 'There' as he did so.

"So what are you doing down on the ground?"

"I," Urska searched around for an explanation, not for any old explanation, but one that could preserve her dignity and not reveal her real situation. "I, haven't been well, and I just was a bit…" But she didn't stand a chance, the humanity and tenderness he offered was too much. She burst into tears and grabbed the shiny-buttoned torso of Officer Wilson.

"It's OK, lady, I got yah," said Officer Wilson.

Urska tried to continue, and Officer Wilson pieced together her words as best as he could. She tore on through her experience at Mario's.

"So," he summed up. "An intelligent lady like you is gonna get upset because some two-bit hash-slinger like Mario said you're a junkie? I've been on these streets for three years and I can see a junkie from ten blocks away."

Urska looked at him. "Really?"

"You bet. Look at you, yeah, I can see you've been sick, you look a little pale, thin maybe, but so what? That happens anyway when you eat at Mario's."

Urska tried to chuckle but instead it just resulted in more tears.

"Furthermore, your watch and clothes are too pricey, junkies always sell those things. Your hair is full of life and soft and your eyes are clear and blue. So take it from an expert, you don't look like a junkie." He smiled deeply, a smile so committed it would have been an insult for Urska not to respond with one of equal splendour. Urska did.

"Can I escort you somewhere?" asked Officer Wilson.

"Maybe, I am looking for the MFA," said Urska as she dried her eyes.

"Museum of Fine Arts?"

"Yes, is it far from here?"

"No, well not by bus. On foot would take you a day, forest roads, long and boring," Officer Wilson closed his umbrella. "You see! The rain's stopped, I'll bet you everything will work out just fine for you."

Urska smiled. "I hope you're right."

The Police at the Leydens

What now? Patricia thought. A patrol car sat in the Leydens' driveway, lights flashing, and crackling voices and bleeps coming over the radio. An officer stood with a clipboard, scribbling away. Standing next to him, of all people, was Mateusz.

The moment the Leydens got out of the car, Mateusz ran up to Patricia. "Have you seen Urska?"

"Hold on, sir" said the officer. "You'll have to wait."

Mateusz turned to the officer. "But it's my girlfriend, I must know if they've seen her."

"Sir! Like I said before," continued the officer, "she's over eighteen, and we cannot file a missing persons report before forty-eight hours. I have her photo, your cell phone, as soon as I can file the report I will, but I cannot do it before, OK?"

"Yes, I understand," said Mateusz. "Which is exactly why I need to ask them if they've seen her."

"Hold on one second, Mateusz," said Patricia calmly.

Mateusz nodded reluctantly as he channelled his frustrations into his body, stiffening it up and turning away from the group.

"What happened?" Daniel asked the officer.

"You had a break-in," said the officer, pointing at the open window. "Actually, a break-out."

"What?" said Daniel.

"Yes, sir, no sign of a forced entry, but the alarm was tripped when that window was opened from the inside. Was anybody inside the house when you left?"

"No," said Daniel.

"You'd better go inside and check to see if anything's missing. I checked inside already, your neighbor, a Mrs...." he looked at his notes, "Corrado gave me the keys, but there is no sign of a burglary. Normally they mess the place up. That doesn't mean that you weren't robbed, however, so as I said, please go on inside and check."

"Come on, honey," said Daniel to Patricia.

"You go on in, I need to speak to Mateusz."

Daniel and the officer made their way to the front door.

Patricia touched Mateusz's shoulder, he had his back to her and turned. "I haven't seen her, did you try to call her?" said Patricia.

"We share one cell phone, this one," he pulled his cell partially out of his jacket pocket. "They're expensive, we're always together so made no sense to have two."

"Hold on just a second," Daniel said to the officer. He walked back down to Patricia and Mateusz. "She came here."

"OK," said Mateusz enthusiastically. "What happened? What did she say? Where did she go?"

"Hey, hey, calm down, calm down," said Daniel holding out a hand. "She was just here for a few minutes, I gave her a camera you left."

"A camera I left?"

"Yes," said Daniel. "You left one down by the laundry door, a night vision something or other."

"OK, what else?" asked Mateusz impatiently.

"Well, nothing, really. Well, she wanted to speak to Patricia."

"To me?" asked Patricia. "What for?"

"It's silly, nonsense," responded Daniel.

"What's silly? What's nonsense?" said Patricia firmly.

"She said we must get rid of the painting," Daniel looked at his feet and then at Patricia.

"And you didn't think to tell me this? Anything else?" asked Patricia.

Daniel shrugged and motioned gestures impossible to decipher.

Patricia lost her patience at this. She growled. "Anything else?"

"OK, OK, she showed me her legs," Daniel paused. "They were covered in scratches."

Mateusz looked at Patricia. "*You* know where those scratches came from."

Daniel interrupted, "Oh damn, here we go again; no, we don't know."

"I'm saying Patricia knows, not *you*," Mateusz shouted.

"Is everything OK over there?" asked the officer.

"Everything's fine, thanks," responded Daniel.

Mateusz continued in a sinister whisper. He pointed at Daniel. "*You* don't know. Patricia does, I do, and Urska does."

Daniel's eyes opened wide in realization. "It was her, Urska! She got in … the painting!" Daniel turned and ran into the house, followed immediately by the officer and then by Patricia and Mateusz.

They arrived at the painting in the same order. Daniel picked up a chrome zippo lighter sitting on the carpet underneath the painting.

"Is this hers?" he asked Mateusz. Mateusz took the lighter from Daniel.

"Yes, this is hers."

"So it's obvious what she was trying to do, come to think of it," Daniel slapped his forehead and smiled. "She asked me if we were both going out."

Mateusz lost control. He leaped forward and grabbed Daniel's shirt. "What the fuck? You think this is funny? You're an asshole, you know that?"

The officer jumped in between them, as did Patricia. But Mateusz wouldn't let go of Daniel's shirt. "She came here to burn that cursed picture and try to release herself from its curse. And you, you smile."

Finally the officer and Patricia managed to prise them apart. Daniel straightened his shirt. He pointed at Mateusz. "Don't call me an asshole just because I don't believe in this nonsense."

"What is going on here?" asked the officer. "So it was your girlfriend, Urska, who was here? Was it *her* who broke in?"

"Yes," said Mateusz dejectedly. "But only to destroy that painting, not to steal anything."

"Do you want to press charges?" the officer asked Daniel and Patricia.

Daniel looked at Mateusz. Then he turned to the officer and asked, "If we press charges, what'll happen?"

The officer understood the hidden question. "We can put out an all-points bulletin, that's to all cars, to apprehend the suspect immediately."

Daniel looked at Mateusz and then back at the officer. "In that case then yes, we want to press charges."

Mateusz bowed his head began to walk down the stairs. Without turning, he said, "Daniel?"

"Yes?" responded Daniel.

"Thanks." He paused and then turned and looked up at Daniel. "I'm sorry for what I said."

"That's OK," said Daniel.

Outside in the driveway, Patricia caught up with Mateusz. "What will you do now?"

"I don't know," said Mateusz. "It's good that the police will now at least try to find her. If I know her, she will have gone to find the artist W. Stoneham. I will too. But she was right, you should get rid of it, you should get rid of it before it hurts your family."

Patricia looked at the house and then at Mateusz. "This whole thing is playing against me. Daniel sees this as a personal principle. He doesn't believe in any of it, so he won't give in. For him to accept this is like surrendering to fantasy; he won't do it."

"And you? Are you still in doubt?"

"You'd better go." Patricia clasped Mateusz's hands. "If anything happens, or we see or hear from Urska, I will call you, OK?"

"OK."

Mateusz got in his van. He rolled down the window.

"I hope you find her," said Patricia.

The Museum of Fine Arts

"We are closing," said the librarian.

"Yes, I know, I will be quick," said Urska.

"I'm sorry, I don't mean 'will be,' I mean we are, literally now, closing."

"Oh, but please, I've travelled all day, I need to find information on W. Stoneham, he—"

The librarian interrupted. "I'm sorry, but you'll have to come back in the morning."

Urska didn't push the point. A plan had already formed and had become Plan A.

"OK," smiled Urska, "I will come back tomorrow, what time do you open?"

"Eight a.m.," beamed the librarian. "Have a good night."

"Thank you, and you too."

Urska walked out through the wooden swinging doors. Once they had stopped swinging, she very carefully pushed one open, just enough to slip back through. She crawled behind a book cart full of stationery. She curled herself into a tiny ball. Her theory was sound: *if I can't see them, they can't see me.*

It worked. The lights began to switch off. *Perfect. Now they really can't see me.*

The librarian and a man walked past the book cart and through the swinging doors, they were busy talking. The keys turned in the door. Urska waited, she heard another door lock further away, and then one final time. *Three doors*, she thought, but she decided to deal with that problem later.

Another problem was that Urska had not brought a flashlight and didn't want to switch on the main lights. The street lamps outside cast some light inside, but the shelving aisles were dark. She walked over to the librarian's desk and began to rummage through the desk drawers. Nothing. She took a desk lamp and placed it on the floor and switched it on. It helped to some degree, though the light was low. Still it was something.

Urska walked along the aisles until she got to S. She peered down, but it was too dark, she wouldn't be able to read much. Nevertheless, she began to walk down the aisle. The names were visible only up until Smith, Matthew Smith, and she was less than halfway down. By her reckoning, Stoneham would be in complete darkness. She walked back to the table.

"Perhaps you could use this?" said a voice from behind Urska.

Urska shrieked and spun around.

"No, no, don't be frightened," said the lady. She held out a flashlight.

"I don't understand," said a confused Urska. "Do you work here?"

"No, no," said the lady. "I'm like you, I make my own hours." She smiled.

Urska smiled too, and took the flashlight. "But don't you need it?"

"No, I already have a book."

"But how will you see to read?" Urska inquired.

"Don't worry, we'll put the lamp back on the table."

Urska was hesitant. "Okay, but I hope they don't catch you, us, I really need to find a particular book."

"Don't worry, I do this all the time, you are more cautious than me," the lady smiled reassuringly at Urska. Urska shrugged her shoulders. "Thanks," she said, and made her way back to aisle S.

"Stock, Stokes, Stom, Storck," Urska paused, finally landing on a thin sliver of a paperback: "Stoneham, William." She grabbed the book and took it back to the desk.

"You found your book?" asked the lady.

"Yes," whispered Urska. She flicked through the pages. "'William Stoneham was born...'"

The lady looked at Urska.

Urska said, "Oops, I'm sorry."

"No, no, it's OK, you read it out loud," the lady said. She closed her book and moved her chair next to Urska's. "So this is the book, this is the man?"

"Yes."

"So why is it so important that you find this book? You know this man?" asked the lady.

"No," Urska sighed. "It's a long story."

Urska smiled and turned back to the small pamphlet. "'William Stoneham was born in 1947, in Boston, Massachusetts. He was given up for adoption at birth, spending his first nine months in a Boston orphanage. His adoptive parents gave him the name Stoneham.' But this is no good, I need to know where he is, where he lives. 'Copyright bestbound printing, 1974.' Oh, this is too old." Urska flicked through the small pamphlet. Each page displayed his artwork.

On the very last page, Urska sat back in her seat and stared.

"The Hands Resist Him, painted by William Stoneham 1972."

The lady stared at the picture.

There was a computer on the desk. Urska ran to it and switched it on. It took some time to boot up.

"You have thought of something?" asked the lady.

"Yes, I know his full name now. Before when I searched, I could only find the eBay sale, nothing else."

Urska tapped the keys with precision. Instantly she knew where he was, and why; finally she had the information she needed. The computer and the light went off.

"They're here," said the lady.

Urska turned to the lady and asked, "Who?"

"You know who is here." The lady grabbed Urska's arm and marched her to the doors.

"There is no time," She pulled at the doors but they were shut tight. She pulled Urska by the wrist, dragging her toward a long window, high above the gray-gloss painted walls. "You must climb up!" She turned and looked back into the darkness. From within this darkness came a cry.

Urska shrieked. "What is that?"

"You must go now!" The lady shouted.

Urska put her foot on the radiator beneath the high window, and then she reached up with her outstretched fingers, her arms fully extended. Again came the foul cry.

The lady pushed Urska. "Go, go," she pleaded.

Urska pulled herself up. She pushed at the window, her right foot held in the lady's shaking hands. A blast of cold air burst into the room as the window bolted upwards. The crying was infernal, the sound of something that did not belong. Urska turned and looked down. Behind the lady were two spectres, hobbling toward her.

Urska could finally see the demonic creatures from the painting, and she screamed automatically. One was the boy with his arms outstretched. The other was the doll, holding a battery tightly in her hands.

Urska crawled out of the window backwards, her eyes fixed on the lady's eye. The lady's desperate hands reached up to Urska. The boy began to embrace her. Her skin began to sink into her face. The boy squeezed her, crying like a child who had been reunited with its mother. Then he stopped abruptly and turned his head up toward Urska in one slow motion. Utterly black eyes penetrated into her, streaming tears of blood. He screamed with rage, a rage so utterly complete that it resonated and vibrated through Urska's skull. Urska fell out of the window.

She scrambled to her feet and ran down the empty street as fast as her shaking legs could take her. Before she had time to assimilate any of the events, she was already far away on a long forest road.

*

The Museum of Fine Arts was an isolated building. The road that seemed only a few minutes by bus when she arrived was now dauntingly endless.

There was no sidewalk. Urska was forced to walk in the road. The road was nothing more than a brutal slice that had carved the forest into two sides. The long thin trees were clumped together closely, very closely, looking as if they had done so out of fear. The evening mist was thick; Urska couldn't see past the first two or three trees in depth.

Behind those trees was the White Mountain National Forest. Enormous, beautiful and deadly, locals say it just takes ten steps to get lost. From a short distance, it seemed the mist had closed the road in front of Urska. But she pushed forward, as she knew the wall of mist was only a trick of the effects of atmosphere. She also knew that the distant footsteps behind her were her own footsteps echoing. The same atmospheric effects playing tricks of sound and reverberation. She could easily test this theory; she could stop and see if the footsteps also stopped. She decided not to do so. She also decided not to ask herself why she had decided not to do so.

In the distance coming toward her were the lights of a vehicle. It was of no use to her. First, it was going in the wrong direction, back to the museum, and second, in this fog the driver would never see her. Her only concern was to stay to her right. In a few moments, this giant from the mist was upon her. The bright lights blurred past her, Urska stopped and tensed. She closed her eyes tightly, bracing herself against the sound of the huge engine which was followed by a blast of cold air the trailer had dragged behind it.

The fleeting mayhem produced by this automotive monster quickly fell back into complete silence as the truck disappeared into the road from whence she had come. She recommenced walking, her echoing footsteps also recommenced walking. But were they nearer? She stopped for a moment. *Maybe if it is something, then it caught up while I stopped?*

Urska pulled her collar up around her chin. She had a permanent chill up her back. Chills are normally momentary and thankfully infrequent, but for Urska her ordeal and the cold air of the evening forest resulted in this permanent sensation, like a tag team to keep the chill 'on'.

The echoing footsteps were clearer and nearer, much nearer. Urska stopped, the footsteps also stopped; they stopped a second after Urska stopped. But this was normal, thought Urska. An echo would do exactly that. *Otherwise it wouldn't be an echo.*

This reasoning was reassuring. In fact, it was so reassuring the tag team of chills was almost about to lose its timing, Urska might even feel her back and neck again, feel them without these pins. Unfortunately, the chill didn't go away. In fact, it became instantly worse. It did so because the echoing footsteps started walking again, even as Urska stood quite still. Then those same footsteps began to run. The moment they did so, so did Urska, she ran, and she ran screaming.

She ran into the thick mist as fast as she could. But what her panic and adrenaline gave her in speed, it took in wisdom. When she could no longer hear the footsteps behind her, she stopped.

So how many trees was that?

She could walk east to Conway or west to Plymouth. Plymouth would be easier, as that's where she was headed anyway, not that she knew, she just needed to turn facing south, and in ten paces she would be back on the road. But even if she did know, which way was south?

I will retrace my steps. And find what was following me? That's stupid.

Urska leaned against a tree. *What to do?* She turned around and pressed her back against the cold, uncaring tree.

She decided she would not move any further, but she would wait for another vehicle to indicate where the road was. And if she froze to death, then she froze to death, she was determined she would face whatever would come, be it death or demons. She sat at the foot of the tree, staring ahead into the mist.

She was aware of every sound, the sounds of nocturnal winter nature. Every twig snapping and every leaf shaking. Among this array of sounds only one sound was of any worry. A twig snapping. It snapped at eleven o'clock from her position, but the difference of this twig from all the others was that two had snapped at this same eleven o'clock space. 'Snap' again, eleven o'clock. Urska realized she wasn't breathing, though she *was*, only very shallowly. 'Snap,' eleven o'clock. *'OK something's there.'*

Urska tried to disappear into the tree. She tried to meditate herself into the wood and the bark. 'Snap,' loud and close. Coming into view through the mist was a small shape. The shape grew nearer and more defined. Two small eyes stared at Urska. The small eyes reflected the dim moonlight, the creature moved toward Urska. Out from the mist it crept into view, a small trembling fox. The fox stared at Urska. *Could this be what was following me? A fox?* prayed Urska.

The fox's ears twitched. Then they twitched again. Then it was Urska's turn to hear what the fox had heard. A vehicle, a truck.

It came closer and closer until it roared behind her. Urska got up and walked through the thick mist toward the streaming lights. She made it back out to the road and continued her walk.

Again she heard the echoing footsteps. She turned, walking backwards without stopping, just behind the wall of mist, the two shining eyes blinked, the pointy ears barely visible.

She turned back. Finally, in the distance she could see an open sided bus shelter.

Once she arrived at this remote outpost, she studied the bus map behind the scratched plastic, she pointed on a place on the map. "OK, so it looks like change here for Binghamton."

The fog closed in around the small bus shelter. Urska placed her backpack on her lap as she sat on the narrow plastic bench, angled on a slope and suspended too high to give any real comfort. The fox tentatively crept in and stood next to the curved metal tubing that supported the shelter. He didn't look at Urska.

Urska knew that this fox was not an incarnation of any demon. Through her ordeal, she had found an untapped fountain of depth, a new language and understanding that could transcend any physical limitations. She could almost speak to this fox. And she did.

If her newfound talents were correct, then this fox was and had been protecting her. The fox, however, did not reciprocate her attempts to connect, not because it didn't want to, but simply because it was too busy. The moment this occurred to Urska, she heard a cry from within the mist. The same cry as she heard in the museum. The fox's ears twitched. It turned in the direction of this cry and responded with its own. The fox arched its back and shrieked out. It did so in that mystical voice that only solitary creatures of the night possess. Its small stomach curved in and upwards with each cry.

Urska didn't need to be a wildlife expert to understand this shrill haunting cry of the fox. It was not a cry of hunger or any mating call or even call to cubs, it was a cry of aggression, and a warning of attack. In human language it would have said, 'You don't scare me, I'll rip your head off if you come any nearer.'

But there was no response, nothing. He cried again.

From within the mist, the flat cry finally responded, the sound of pain, but the pain of many. This demon hidden behind a veil of mist didn't seem to be the possessor of these sounds, as no one thing could produce such sounds, but it seemed to be more a portal, a portal that carried lost voices from some unspeakable place to this place, now, here, on this lonely forest road. In the seconds it had remained silent it had grown nearer, now it came from just behind the heaving wall of mist. The fox adopted an aggressive stance. Urska stood up and backed into the corner of the shelter, covering her ears from this abominable sound.

The fox ran out instantly in the direction of whatever it was, disappearing into the mist.

A savage frenzy of cries and growls burst into the air, like a fight between two mythical beasts. Shrill roars that sounded like ripping and tearing. A fight to the death. Then silence. The energy of this fight visible in the swirls and shapes in the mist.

Urska sank down and curled into the corner of the shelter. She didn't blink, she kept her eyes fixed on the dense curtain. Her fate depended on who or what emerged from it.

Something emerged.

Two small, outstretched arms reached out from behind the wall of mist. The foul cry recommenced, breaking the still air. Urska screamed sharply as the boy drifted into view, behind him the small outline of his pernicious companion staggered into view.

He looked at Urska, his eyes begging. He cried out for her embrace. Urska stood up and shook her head. "No, no, get back!" She screamed.

She knew she couldn't go with them, she didn't know where it was but she had heard it, through his screams, she had heard it. The boy threw his arms down by his sides and clenched his fists, he began to shake violently, the pale skin of his eye lids blinked over his black eyeballs, squeezing blood from each side.

Urska began swinging her bag in front of her as she staggered out of the shelter.

The boy reached his arms out again, beckoning for his deadly embrace, screaming at Urska, demanding her affection. Urska collapsed to the ground, her thin legs unable to stand anymore.

He reached down toward Urska's thin, defeated face.

Urska saw a bright light, it grew larger and nearer, it began to consume her entire view. She recognized this light, she had heard it mentioned many times before, she began to surrender herself to it. As it fell upon her, this brilliant light engulfed both demons from her vision, the damnable crying was also engulfed, engulfed by a sound even louder, the sound of a diesel engine. The doors hissed open.

"What are you doing on the ground?" said the bus driver, smiling down at Urska. Urska was amazed that she was still alive; so amazed that she hesitated, and she looked around, bewildered. Finally, she picked herself up in a daze and climbed onto the bus. "Wow this is thick," he continued, politely not pursuing the question as to why she was on the ground. "I almost went past you. If it wasn't for that dead fox … my lights picked up his green eyes, that's how I know it's a fox, they're the only animal whose eyes reflect green." He smiled at Urska, timing it in an unfortunate contrast to the hiss of the closing doors.

"It looks like he was looking out for yah, huh?"

Good Night, Hector

Gomez was asleep. He was lying on the crime scene photographs, which were spread out over the dining room table, some of them placed upright in a fruit bowl, one balanced against an orange and one held between four bananas like the old coin trick.

His mother gently shook his right shoulder. "Hector," she whispered.

Gomez began to wake. He sat up with a photograph stuck to his face. "Ma? I must have fallen asleep." Gomez slowly got up from the creaking chair, he kissed his mother on the forehead. She smiled and peeled the photograph from his cheek. He peered toward the black windows.

"Wow, I really did sleep." He looked at his watch, it was almost eleven p.m. "Good night, Ma."

"Good night, Hector."

Gomez left the room. Mrs. Gomez stared, concerned, at her son. Then she sat down at the table and began to collect the photographs, starting by pulling one free from the banana fingers in the fruit bowl. Trying her best to avoid looking at them, she tried to look around them and not really focus, but slowly they engaged her.

Enigmistica

Gomez peered out of the kitchen window onto a fresh Boston morning. He stirred his coffee as he walked through into the dining room. He saw his mother at the table; she was asleep, lying on the photos. He intensified the jingling of the teaspoon against the mug.

"Ma! Wake up. So it's your turn to sleep on those things."

Mrs. Gomez awoke, fully excited. This took Gomez by surprise.

"Hector, Hector, take a look," Mrs. Gomez placed two of the photographs side by side on the table. Gomez looked at his mother, then back at the photographs on the table. She continued, "Well?"

"Well, what? You shouldn't be looking at those," Gomez said, pointing at her with his spoon.

"But take a look, Hector." Gomez pretended to look at each of them, but his uninterested eyes betrayed him. "You're not even looking," she said impatiently, pointing directly at one photograph.

"Look!" The photograph showed a large reception area, with the outline of a body taped on the floor, above which hung a painting.

"What?" said a pressurized Gomez. "I don't see anything special."

"OK, look at this one," Mrs. Gomez remained smiling with excitement.

In the second photograph in the background heavily out of focus there was a blank spot where a painting used to hang.

Mrs. Gomez waved her hands at him dismissively. "It's not what you see, it's what you don't see." She walked over to her knitting bag and came back with a knitting needle. She pointed at the first photograph with the tip of the metal knitting needle. "Look at this painting." She moved the needle to the left over the second crime scene photograph. "This, this space on the wall, a painting was there, no? And it looks to be the same size."

Gomez's eyes opened wide. His mother, on seeing his reaction, smiled.

"Ah, now you see, now you see."

Gomez was stunned. He dropped his spoon into his empty cup and placed it hastily on the table. He stared at his mother, who very contentedly smiled back. "Enigmistica."

Gomez nodded and repeated in a whisper, "Enigmistica." Gomez grabbed the photos and held them up. "Could be, could be, you never know."

*

Gomez burst out the door with one arm in his jacket, his case file stuffed in a leather satchel and the two photos between his lips. He made his way to his car and got in. He placed the two photographs face down, on each knee. "Peabody '76 and Johnson '97". He went through the files. "Peabody, Peabody." Rain was pouring heavily on the windshield as the wipers flashed back and forth. He turned on the fan, which blew out some dried leaves, a small particle of which went straight into his eye. "Ow, shit!" He closed it and continued his search with his right eye. He pulled out a stapled set of five pages titled "Peabody '76." He placed it on the passenger seat and immediately recommenced his search. As his left eye started to water, he finally found the Johnson file, which he placed on top of Peabody.

Gomez blinked his eye into submission. He could see, he had both case files and the windshield had cleared. He was good to go.

The Shop

Dyson Von Bilbow Apsland stood, half-bathed in a yellow light. It could be called "radiation yellow," as it had a nuclear tinge to it. The dark-panelled wooden walls were, at the least, unusual. He couldn't remember why he was even there, did he forget something, milk maybe, bread? But this wasn't a grocery store. Sitting next to an impressive cast-iron cash register was a cloth frog holding a silver flute, there were tin soldiers and ceramic animals, in a glass cabinet lay square tiles of immaculate lead soldiers. All of these items, as old as they were, were in incredible condition. Like new, in fact.

Apsland called out, "Hello?" His voice fell flat. It didn't travel any distance at all, he was aware his feet were touching the wooden floor, yet he couldn't feel them. He turned toward the door. Small squares of dusty glass containing tiny air bubbles filled the windows. Through them shone the yellow light, peering through, he didn't recognize the street. There were no houses, just a dry tree and an abandoned child's homemade go-cart. Nothing moved in its yellow atmosphere. He wiped away some of the dust on one of the glass tiles. He peered through as close as he could, as he looked out, a combination of the glass and the yellow light had a strange effect, an odd elusion, the tree and the go-cart, and everything else he could see seemed like it was set inside the same yellow glass, like a flower set in a glass paperweight.

He turned to his right and looked down to the end of a dark corridor. He called out again, "Hello?" In answer, a small white face peered from the darkness. Apsland physically bolted backwards. "Hello?" he cried out. The small white face took another step, a step revealing to Apsland what it was: a doll. This doll, however, did not lie on its back motionless, this doll was no typical inanimate toy. This doll was walking toward him, she held something in her hands, she was looking directly at him, in him, and she did so without eyes.

Apsland broke away, he turned toward the door and grabbed the door handle, but he stopped and relaxed his tense grip, and then slowly turned back to the doll. She had disappeared back into the dark corridor.

He searched to keep her in view, the dark sockets of her eyeless eyes beckoned he should follow. He still couldn't feel the floor, as if he had set the gravity switch to neutral.

He entered the dark corridor, led by his own curiosity. His hands touched the dark-panelled wooden walls. As he progressed, the corridor became shorter and narrower. The doll had disappeared into the long narrow tunnel. Apsland, to his own amazement, called to her to wait, but she was gone. He could go no further, he could see nothing, he was curled to almost half his height and his torso twisted. His breathing was becoming laboured. He pulled at his collar, he was aware he was consciously avoiding panic. His breathing was getting shorter and quicker, and so he closed his eyes. "Calm, calm, OM. *Tryambakam yajamahe Sugandhim pushti-vardhanam.*" He continued his chant through sweating lips.

He became aware of something shuffling at speed toward him. He stopped chanting and opened his eyes. But this wasn't the doll. This time there was anger in the pace, more than anger, rage; a rage so violent, it was rendering its host incapable of efficiency in movement. Apsland turned back, but the path he had taken was now too shrunken for him to return. He continued to chant, but the chanting was like no other chant, such gentle ancient words screamed in such terror.

The corridor was now so small that Apsland was forced to lie flat, and the wooden ceiling was inches from his face. He tried to wriggle back down but there was a panel in place below his feet was, and another above his head. The crazed shuffling was almost upon him, and he began to scream; he kicked and punched at the wooden ceiling with his knees and hands. It began to give, he pushed, employing unknown muscles and energy sources that he had never used before. He sat up, still holding the ceiling, but it wasn't a ceiling, it was a lid, he was sitting in a coffin. A coffin suspended on a large table and draped with a red velvet cloth. Above him was a single light, separating him from an eternal darkness.

From this darkness, a black soundless sea of shapes writhed like an enormous grotesque insect queen, and from this queen, individual shapes began to tentatively emerge. Slowly from the darkness, the ghostly murmuring shapes became visible, each doomed captive had suffered horrific mutilations that should have rendered them lifeless, yet they lived. They reached out decomposing white arms to Apsland. Apsland was surrounded, the chance of salvation had excited these tortured souls, their dull murmurs now rising to desperate pleas of rescue.

"Apsland, Apsland … Apsland, hey!"

Apsland crumbled to the floor, knocking over a lava lamp. Gomez fell to his knees to help Apsland.

"God, Apsland, are you OK?"

Apsland sat up, drool dripped from his mouth. He stared at Gomez with the same vacant eyes as an epileptic when fitting. Gomez sat Apsland back against the bottom of an armchair.

"Your door was open."

Apsland wiped his mouth with his sleeve and grabbed Gomez's wrists. They both stood up together. A concerned Gomez stared back at Apsland, searching for an explanation. Finally, Apsland released Gomez's wrists.

"Do you want some water?" asked Gomez.

Apsland coughed and pointed a trembling finger. "Get me that whiskey, over there."

Gomez got up and walked over to a 1960's refrigerator, on top of which was a bottle. Gomez picked up the bottle and looked around.

"Don't worry about a glass," ordered Apsland. "Hand it here." Apsland clambered into his armchair and poured at least three doubles directly in his mouth.

"What happened?" asked Gomez.

The dream had provided Apsland with no useful information.

"Nothing, bad dream, bad dream," said Apsland, wiping his sweaty eyes.

"I need to check something out," said Gomez. "Do you want to come?"

"What is it?" asked Apsland.

"A long shot is what it is, but nevertheless, I have to check it, well, rule it out, if anything," Gomez looked at Apsland. "Two crime scene photos, twenty-one years apart, one, has a painting on the wall, the other a white space where a painting used to hang. Yeah, long shot, but I have to say the dimensions look the same, so I just need to rule it out."

The whiskey had worked its magic; Apsland was finally relaxed.

Gomez continued, "It's a weird painting, it's of a boy and a doll, outside—"

"Of a shop!" interrupted Apsland.

Gomez said, "Ah, so you remember the photo?"

Apsland didn't answer.

Peabody

Apsland and Gomez stood outside of an Art Deco condominium
block. They could tell that it was a beauty back in the day; the block
bore the same honest beauty as an aging starlet who refused plastic
surgery.

"Seventeen," said Gomez. They made their way up to the
second floor and walked along the corridors. Down the hallway there
was a row of doormats of all shapes, size and color. Each door was
constrained from expressing individuality in any way. Only the door
mats could attempt to do that. One apartment did stand out, however.
It was the only apartment without a doormat.

They headed towards that apartment, it was beyond any
doubt that this would be Number Seventeen.

Of course it was. Seventeen had no curtains either, just black
bin liners covering the walls.

Gomez tapped at the door. They waited in silence. He
pressed the buzzer, but it didn't sound, so he knocked harder.

"There ain't nobody home." A thin elderly black lady was peering out from Number Sixteen.

"Ma'am," said Gomez. "It's empty?"

"That's right," she said "Been empty for about a year now."

"Ma'am," Gomez turned to Apsland and back again to the neighbor. "Ma'am, I am Detective Hector Gomez from Boston PD, this is Mr. Apsland."

Apsland reached out his hand to the neighbor. "My pleasure, madam."

Gomez displayed his badge, and the elderly neighbor placed her hand over her chest.

"Please don't be alarmed," continued Gomez. "Have you lived in your apartment for many years?"

"Since '63."

"Could we ask you a few questions?"

The elderly neighbor indicated to Gomez to hand her his badge. He did so, and she inspected it closely in silence. "Well, come on in."

Apsland wiped his feet on the mat, which read: "Start life together in sunny weather, Florida the Sunshine State."

"Are you from Florida, madam?" asked Apsland courteously to break the ice on entering the house.

"No," she replied. "Just the mat."

The elderly neighbor picked up her television remote with hands that were slightly crooked from arthritis. She muted her television. "I can catch up with Judge Judy some other time," she smiled. "Please take a seat."

"Thank you, ma'am," responded Gomez.

"Please, call me Helen, all of this 'ma'am' and 'madam' is making me feel like an old lady."

The room was awash with color and tropical ornaments, the most impressive of which was a large ceramic toucan sitting on top of a stack of videos.

"Nice place you've got here," smiled Gomez.

"Thank you." She smiled back. "What is it you wanna know?"

"Ma'am, excuse me, Helen, please tell us something about Mr. Sexton."

Helen's eyes dropped. "Poor Mr. Sexton, Harry, I should say." She sighed. "That was all twenty years ago?"

"Yes, it certainly was," replied Gomez. "But the case is still open, unsolved, so we are re-investigating."

Helen shrugged her shoulders. "OK, well, Harry, he was the best neighbor you could have. He had split from his wife, she was already gone when we moved into the complex, me and my dear Windsor, fresh from our honeymoon in Florida. The hotel gave us five of those doormats." She smiled gently at Apsland. "I'm on the fifth one." She nodded to a picture of herself and her late husband, a George Foreman-lookalike. "That's Windsor and me. Harry used to come over on occasion, and we'd talk and talk, he travelled a lot and always brought us back something, even that toucan you was looking at, that was him, nice guy all over, through and through."

Gomez asked, "So when the body turned up, next door, what did you think?"

"We knew it wasn't him." Helen's expression turned to one of disgust. "But he was as good as guilty to everyone, and no disrespect to you, Detective, but the police, when they went after him, they went after him like he was for sure the killer. I almost hoped he got away. Windsor would say to me, I hope he done hightailed it out of Dodge. My man Windsor could see through people like they was made o' glass, and he trusted Harry."

Gomez handed Helen both crime scene photographs. "I guess it's all changed in there now."

Helen looked at the photographs. "Yes, the landlord got someone in there within a month, there's been people in there going and coming for these last twenty years." She handed one back to Gomez. "This ain't his apartment." As Gomez was about to take it back, she snatched it back again. "It ain't his apartment, but that *is* his painting."

"Hot damn!" Gomez slapped his thighs. "Excuse me, Helen."

"What's up? Something I said about the painting?"

"Yes, Helen." Gomez stood up. "Please go on."

"Well, he had this thing on his wall. We hardly ever went into his place, but I remember it, I remember because it was a strange thing. I don't spook easily but this thing was creepy. Windsor was talking to Harry on the landing one morning, in fact, not long before the day of the murder, and I just heard Windsor say, 'You ain't getting no sleep cos o' that ugly-ass picture you done hung on the wall,' or words to that effect."

"He couldn't get any sleep?" asked Gomez.

"I don't think so," Helen shook her head. "That's what Windsor said, so I guess not. Come to think of it, he did look awful around that time, tired, worried."

Gomez waved the photograph nervously. "I don't suppose he ever told you the artist or the title, did he?"

"No," she replied. "Is it important?"

"No, I'll just get them to blow up a negative, then we should be able to read the signature."

Apsland asked, "Do you know what happened to the painting?"

"No, sir." Helen stood up as they all motioned toward the door. "They found Harry like Peabody was found, huh?"

Gomez nodded reluctantly. "Yes, Helen, I'm afraid they did."

She opened the door. "All cut up like him, like Peabody." She shook her head. "Poor Harry. God bless his soul."

*

Gomez and Apsland made their way out of the building. They stood beside Gomez's car.

"Hang on, Apsland." Gomez called the precinct on his cell phone as he sat against the front left fender. Apsland took the opportunity to fill his pipe.

"Who's this? Tom, it's Gomez, is the captain there?" He looked at the pictures and chuckled, then he heard the captain on the line. The ancient precinct telephone exchange reduced O'Hara's booming voice to a hollow, cheap imitation.

"Captain," said Gomez. "The 1997 case file, Laura Johnson, and the 1976 case, Peabody, we've identified that in Harry Sexton's home, where Peabody was found and in Harriet McKenzie's, where Laura Johnson was found, was the same item, a painting. Now, I know it's not much, but over twenty years separates those two cases."

The captain soberly pointed out that it could be a print of a famous piece. "It's not that tennis chick scratching her ass, is it?" asked O'Hara.

Gomez ignored the gag but heeded the message. "I don't think it's famous, but anyway it's something. I'm with Apsland now, and we're going over to the Catskills to speak to the widower of Harriet McKenzie. Maybe he can shed some light on this. Meanwhile, can I ask a favor?"

"Anything," responded the small tinny voice.

"I need someone to visit the residences on file pertinent to the case and ask if any of the residents or friends of the victims have been in possession of this painting or know of it." Gomez listened to O'Hara, and he turned over the first photograph. "Yeah, it's from negative 7790998, we need to be able to read the signature. By the way, it's not that tennis chick scratching her ass, Captain, it's of a boy and what looks like maybe a doll standing outside a shop. It's a creepy bastard thing, Captain. Oh, and Captain?"

"What is it?" replied the tinny voice.

Gomez took a breath. "The doll in the painting doesn't appear to have any eyes."

Captain O'Hara said nothing. This silence told Gomez as much as any words. The captain was interested. He finally spoke. "Gomez. Good work."

"Thanks, Captain, but it wasn't me."

"Who was it? Don't tell me Apsland was of use?"

"My ma," responded Gomez.

"Your mother?" said O'Hara.

"Yeah, she's always playing those spot-the-difference games."

"Tell her she'll be up for a citizen's award if we nail this bastard."

"Thanks, Captain, will do."

The Spider

Captain O'Hara hung up the phone and pondered, staring into the distance. He broke himself away and snapped, "McCabe."

Detective McCabe was busy consoling a prostitute he was about to book. "Hold on, sugar, I'll be back."

McCabe took his beer gut over to the captain. "What?"

"What the hell is Deirdre doing back in here?" grumbled O'Hara.

"She missed you, she got herself booked to catch a glimpse of you."

"We don't have time, get her out of here. I need you and Marvin."

McCabe leaned forward. "I can't."

"Why the hell not?"

McCabe flicked his eyes over to Marvin Hamilton's desk. Marvin was busy taking a statement from a Mr. Braithwaite, who was proudly sporting an indecently dirty collar and clutching a stack of small, stiff papers.

"Oh, shit," said O'Hara. "So that's why you brought her in: Braithwaite!"

McCabe shrugged apologetically. "He states she propositioned him."

"What the hell's wrong with that? At his age it's a compliment, and for that cockroach a miracle."

"He says he was handing out flyers for his pawn shop and she made…" McCabe looked at his notes, "'a lewd and suggestive remark to me in front of my wife.'"

O'Hara smiled and waved his finger. "Ah, now I get it, his wife was there, so he's showing his disgust, making a point, showing he has been off-en-deeeeeed. You see, McCabe, even a cockroach can be off-en-deeeeeed."

O'Hara walked over to Marvin Hamilton's desk. "Excuse me for a moment, Marvin."

O'Hara sat on the edge of Marvin's desk and shook Mr. Braithwaite's hand with great respect. "Mr. B." O'Hara smiled insincerely at Mr. Braithwaite with all of his teeth.

"Captain O'Hara," Mr. Braithwaite responded nervously.

"Mr. B, did you sign the statement yet?"

"No, but I am about to, and nothing you can say will stop me."

O'Hara turned to Marvin. "Did you hear that, Marvin?"

"I sure did," said Marvin as he tapped and coiled his pen on the desk.

"This is the type of citizen we need."

"I hear that, Captain."

O'Hara leaned forward and straightened Mr. Braithwaite's tie. "Even though Mr. Braithwaite knows that in court, Ms. Washington will refute these claims, even though half the neighborhood will be there, even though Mr. Braithwaite will be expected to repeat what Ms. Washington allegedly said, er, what was that?"

Marvin began to read: "Deirdre, also known..."

"No, no, Marvin, let's hear it from Mr. Beeeeeee." O'Hara looked at Mr. Braithwaite. "After all, you're the one who's been off-en-deeeeeeed, aren't you? Please go ahead, read. I'll close my eyes."

Marvin held out the statement to Mr. Braithwaite, who looked at Marvin furiously. "Braithwaite to you. Anyway I don't want it to read the allegation! What the shit?"

O'Hara opened his eyes, and looked at Mr. Braithwaite in disgust. "Read it."

Mr. Braithwaite reluctantly took the paper from Marvin. "You know, you're a bully, O'Hara. One day…" he began to stutter. "One day, well, anyway, a civilian outranks the police, remember that."

"Read it," growled O'Hara.

Mr. Braithwaite threw the paper back at Marvin. Marvin picked it up and looked at the captain, unsure what to do. Captain O'Hara turned to Marvin.

"I don't get it, he said what she said to you, so why so shy?"

Mr. Braithwaite slammed his hand down on the desk. "You're a bastard, you know that, O'Hara?"

O'Hara chuckled. "OK, I'll read it, Mr. Beeeeeee." He gently pulled the paper from Marvin's fingers, and loudly cleared his throat. He kept doing this until he had the attention of the whole floor, including Deirdre. She sat, wearing purple feathers and scuffed red shiny shoes, looking like a faded Dorothy who had to pay her way out of Oz the hard way.

"Deirdre, also known as Deirdre BOGOF…" O'Hara looked over at Deirdre.

"Deirdre, honey, what's BOGOF?"

An unseen male voice from the back of the room shouted, "Captain O'Hara, sir, that stands for 'Buy One Get One Free.'"

Deirdre just smiled. She tried to wipe her sweating brow and control her trembling lips as she discreetly fought off her looming demons. They were getting hungry, she'd been in the precinct for three hours.

Chuckles rippled around the room. An assortment of detectives, lawyers and criminals listened to the captain's recitation. It was as close to, and as far away from, school story time on the carpet as was possible. The similarities were equally fascinating and disturbing.

"Oh I see, and I always thought that was just a last name, I'm so naive. Thank you, I shall continue, BOGOF, of course you won't have to read that part Mr. Beeeeeee." O'Hara indulged in some laughter at this patronizing reassurance. He continued, and continued the mockery by placing his thumb in his left belt loop and leaning backwards, imitating a 17th-century barrister at London's Old Bailey, to the point where he adopted a comical English accent while reading Mr. Braithwaite's words. "'Ah, here you are, I handed out my flyers, I didn't realize I had handed one to her. She said, "OK you've given me one, how would you like me to give you one? Come on down the alley and I'll take you to heaven." To this I replied, I would like to state I do not and will never enter into any illicit activities with a women selling sexual services.'"

This unlikely response blew the entire office into laughter; even starched lawyers' shirts began to crease. In among it all, the defiant voice of Mr. Braithwaite finally made itself heard.

"I don't care, I don't care, I'll still say it, I don't care who hears it."

O'Hara tipped an invisible hat at Mr. Braithwaite, and looked around the room, smiling enthusiastically like an old Wild West doctor selling a bottle of miraculous formula.

"Even though Ms. Washington makes no literal reference to a sexual act, but merely suggests taking Mr. Braithwaite to heaven, with this, Mr. Braithwaite is still gonna take his chances in court.

What a guy, what a pillar of our community. Ladies and gentlemen, I give you Mr. Braithwaite." O'Hara began a round of applause for Mr. Braithwaite that was unenthusiastically picked up by two seals. Mr. Braithwaite stuck his middle finger at O'Hara.

O'Hara's smile fell. "McCabe, read yours."

"What?" asked Mr. Braithwaite.

O'Hara put an unlit cigar in his mouth. "Mr. B, Ms. Washington here, she has the right of response. Detective McCabe, please read out Ms. Washington's statement."

McCabe responded, "Ah, you read it, Captain, I can't do it like you."

"No, you go ahead."

McCabe walked back over to Deirdre and placed his hand on her shoulder. "'So the spider handed me a flyer...'"

O'Hara took his unlit cigar out of his mouth as he feigned ignorance. "The Spider?"

"Yes sir, it's a nomenclature," smirked McCabe.

O'Hara nodded at McCabe with respect. "A 'nomenclature', you dog," he said, and winked.

Mr. Braithwaite squirmed in his seat.

McCabe cleared his throat but Deirdre broke in, speaking with a sober innocence.   "We call him that, cos when you go in, he can take one look at you and decide paper or powder, but he'll give you what you need, for whatever it is you is in there to sell, and he's gotcha, and he's gonna wrap you up and eat you up a little bit at a time."

Mr. Braithwaite folded his arms and focused his eyes laser-like at the ceiling. "There's a boatful of lawyers in here, I'll sue you for slander."

"You do that!" snapped Deirdre. "And when they come to take my television, they can go straight to your shop, that's where it's at."

O'Hara stood up. "OK, enough now. McCabe, get to it."

McCabe started up again. "'The Spider handed me a flyer, and as a business woman and an entrepreneur I saw a business opportunity.'" O'Hara blew Deirdre a kiss that she didn't see. "'I asked him if he'd pay me to hand out the leaflets for him, he said 'a job?' like it was a stupid idea. Then he laughed, and said 'The only job you can do for me is a blow job,' and then he laughed more, but he didn't know his wife was on him, she heard the whole thing. And when I said no, I wouldn't do it, no one would do it for the Spider, that's when he started yelling. That's when they both started yelling, him at me, her at him, then the police came and all, and it's like that! You know I'm sayin'? Like that!'"

A silence fell, and uneasy embarrassment. Mr. Braithwaite got up from his seat, trembling with silent rage. He shuffled toward the door on his stiff thin legs. Finally he turned. He unwisely made an attempt to recover some dignity but he just dug deeper, way deeper.

"I'm not gonna have no hooker junkie bitch tarnish my good reputation in public. How dare you! How dare you!" No one responded. He gave O'Hara the finger again, and O'Hara responded with a thumbs-up.

The moment Braithwaite left, the room broke into muttered conversation. Marvin smiled as he tore up Braithwaite's statement.

Deidre ran up to O'Hara and threw her bony arms around him. "You're just the champ."

O'Hara blotted her sweaty brow with his tie. "Now get out of here, and go easy on that…" he pointed his finger and swivelled his hand, "…stuff."

Deirdre headed back to Oz with a fragile smile, still clinging to the hope of spotting a balloon with which to make her escape.

McCabe looked down at his beer gut and stroked it. "So all that to free up me and Marv, must be something big?"

"Are you talking about me or the baby in there?" O'Hara quipped.

McCabe raised both eyebrows as if hearing an amazing fact and replied, "I like that, the old ones are the best ones, huh?" he punctuated his comeback with a slick display of dexterity, in a half-second blur he snapped both his fingers, slapped his hands, and pointed both index fingers at O'Hara like revolvers.

O'Hara ignored the pinky guns. "Not big, but you need to help out Gomez, it's an errand, besides I hate that cockroach Braithwaite."

"Geez, you hate him, no kidding? We didn't notice, not me nor absolutely every single person in the room."

"OK get going," said O'Hara.

"Where?" asked McCabe.

"Oh yeah, right," said O'Hara. "Marvin!" he yelled. "Get over here."

"Yes, Captain," responded Marvin from behind his green ceramic lamp.

O'Hara got up and walked over to his office, a wooden and glass room within the main floor.

"Oh would ya look at this, Marvin, hey look at this everybody, me and Marvin are going into the office, cos we're special," said McCabe, churning it up for fun.

O'Hara, Marvin and McCabe made their way into the room.

Marvin waved his hand in front of his face. "Wow, it smells kinda stale in here."

"It is stale," said McCabe. "Stale in air and stale in style, which incidentally is distressed 1930's. Captain, our Captain O'Hara, doesn't use this office much, do ya, Cap?"

"Nope," responded O'Hara as he swivelled around some chairs and wheeled them toward Marvin and McCabe. He made his way to each blind and zig-zagged them from left to right as they inched their way up. He pulled at the tarnished brass loops at the foot of the wooden window frames, and inched them up in a similar zig-zag fashion. "That'll let out the stale air a bit," said O'Hara.

"Not only do our blinds open up like that," said McCabe. He held out his hands, raising one hand up, then the other until he levelled them out at about shoulder height. "But even our windows, they all work like that."

"So does McCabe," laughed O'Hara, and he made the same gesticulations that McCabe had just finished. "He works like that too." They all laughed. No one really understood the gag, including O'Hara, but it was funny nevertheless.

"You know why I never come in here, Marvin?" said O'Hara.

"No, sir?" said Marvin.

"Oh no, here we go again," said McCabe. "Am I gonna have to stand and salute as usual?"

O'Hara looked at McCabe through the corner of his eye and then looked at Marvin. "Marvin," said O'Hara. "It's because out there," he peered through the blinds into the outer office, "out there, there's a kind of…" he inhaled through his nostrils. "Air."

"I'll say," interjected McCabe.

O'Hara continued ignoring McCabe's heckling. "In here, yeah of course, I could swivel in this chair," which he did, he rotated

360 degrees and then continued. "And feel all big and yada-yada, but I like to be out there with you guys, a finger on the pulse, not in here surrounded with all the trappings of success."

Marvin looked at McCabe.

"You did it again, Captain," said McCabe. "Look at poor Marvin, he doesn't know if you're serious or not."

O'Hara clapped his hands, signalling an end to his antics, if that's what they were, of course.

"McCabe," said O'Hara.

"Yes, sir," responded McCabe. McCabe knew when to joke around and when not to. That was an achievement O'Hara particularly prided in his detectives. He always knew someone would be where he wanted them when he passed the ball.

"I want you and Marvin to go through the victims list of the Life Swapper case, Gomez's case. Take that list and locate any living relative who lived with or visited the victim at the time of their disappearance, and if you have them, also contact known associates of the victims," said O'Hara.

"And from that list we should ask them…?" asked McCabe.

"If they ever saw this painting." O'Hara pushed a small photograph along the desk and rotated it in their direction. McCabe and Marvin got up from their swivel chairs.

"It's pretty small," said Marvin squinting.

"Yeah, that reminds me, get this blown up, the number's on the back." Captain O'Hara flipped it over. "7790998." O'Hara rustled around in a drawer and came up with a magnifying glass. He handed it to Marvin. Marvin looked over the photograph through the magnifying glass. Then the glass fell out of its metal loop and landed on the photo. Marvin looked up at the captain apologetically.

McCabe pointed at it. "That's a trapping of success, that."

Marvin picked it up directly without putting it back in its frame. He studied the photo. "What the hell is that, Captain? A doll?"

"Yeah," O'Hara said, and placed his hands behind his head. "You're familiar with the case, right?"

"Sure," responded Marvin. "It was Manfreddi's." Marvin looked back at the photograph and then looked back up at O'Hara. "The eyes, right? On the doll, no eyes? Something there? With that?"

"Maybe," said O'Hara. "Gomez has discovered that this painting was owned by two of the victims, and there's twenty years between each death."

McCabe nodded at O'Hara seriously. "We get it, Captain, we're on it. Marv, let's go."

The Bus Terminal

"Miss, Miss?"

Urska was curled into a ball. She opened her sticky eyes. A handsome station guard peered down at her.

"Sorry I have to wake you up, people are starting to arrive." He smiled.

Urska immediately obeyed and sat up.

"I let you sleep," he continued. "Because no one was here. These bus terminals don't like people sleeping on the seats, but you looked like you needed it so I left you alone."

Urska smiled back. "Thank you very much. You're right, I haven't slept properly for a while."

"Where are you headed?"

"Binghamton."

"Ah, OK." He looked at his watch. "Just another fifteen minutes or thereabouts."

"Yes," replied Urska. "I think it leaves at seven, right? I'm so lucky you woke me, thanks."

"That's right, on both counts." He winked.

"Are you OK for food? There's a vending machine at the entrance."

"OK, thanks, if I feel hungry I will get something, thank you again."

"My pleasure, miss, have a safe journey."

Urska wanted to be rid of him. He was nice and helpful, plus she was having a normal conversation, but she felt stripped, she felt naked, the events of the last few days had left her feeling a mere shell of her true self. Eventually through some elimination of possible reasons, she finally realized the reason she didn't want to talk to him. She was quite shocked to admit to herself the reason was simple: embarrassment. *Maybe because he is handsome?* The insult from the diner had affected her badly. She was dishevelled, thin, and wore her stress everywhere, for the world to see. Even now, she was garnering curious glances from the corners of eyes. So it was simple ego, she thought, ego! How strong it is, even now, through all this, she still had time for an ego.

She watched the large clock suspended on the brick wall. She caressed her backpack as it sat on her lap. She noticed the lump that was the infrared camera she had placed in the front pouch. She took it out and started to flick through the images on the small LCD screen.

They were all shots of the Leydens' laundry room. All the same. She clicked on through seven or eight. Then she paused and wondered. Why did the camera even take a picture if nothing was there? So she flicked back to the first image. There were two small balls of very faint light, like raindrops on a lens. She knew these as orbs. Paranormal investigators normally consider these as possible manifestations of a supernatural force.

She clicked on, and again, there they were, the timestamp showed that the camera had taken these shots in quick succession. These were the same orbs. As she clicked on, in steady succession, she followed the behaviour of these two spheres. They sat down low and hovered, and then they drew nearer to the camera. She clicked ahead, the door opened, and so did Urska's mouth. She knew the lady who stood in the doorway, she was the lady from the library. Now, on the small LCD screen, there she stood holding a bucket, dropping a bucket. Urska remembered the conversation with Daniel. 'A heart attack … our housekeeper.'

Urska tensed. Her thumb hovered as it sat over the button. She clicked. She watched Manuela's tormented last moments. The last frame was obscured by the two orbs, which were covering her death mask. Urska reflected, she understood that this lady, this dead lady had tried to help her, what place did they take her to? Or were they taking her back somewhere?

Deep in thought, haunted thought, Urska started. She looked up at the large industrial clock. It was time to catch her bus. She stood up and buttoned her jacket. Her stomach heaved. *No, please.* Urska tried to compose herself and get to the toilets as fast as she could without causing a scene. She marched determinedly down the hallway. She could see the sign for the rest room, she was almost there. Almost wasn't good enough. Her tiny stomach heaved. The vomit flew out of her mouth and nose. She stopped dead in her tracks. The waiting passengers no longer looked from the corner of their eyes but directly at her. Their preconceptions of Urska were right, of course, now the junkie was throwing up, and they let her know. The room filled with gasps and mutterings as they berated and condemned her, these superior kings and queens indulged themselves as they cast their cruel comments from their invisible thrones of superiority.

One lady had curled her legs up on her seat as Urska's vomit had just missed her.   Urska with her composure secured in a neck lock walked around her vomit and continued her confident walk toward the large swinging doors as if nothing had happened. The moment she passed through the doors she burst into tears.

The security guard ran up to her as she walked out into the gray morning.

"Are you OK? What's wrong?"

"Nothing!" Urska snapped. "Nothing! Leave me alone." He was more than a little surprised by her reaction, but screams from the waiting room told him his presence was needed elsewhere. Urska looked at him. She knew what the screams were about, and he knew she knew, but he chose to run inside.

Once inside, he met with a crowd of stunned passengers, all looking at the floor.

"Holy shit!" said the guard. After a few seconds of study, he continued, "Maybe she went to an Asian restaurant? They've been known to serve eyes."

The lady with the curled legs now sat up high on the back of the seat.

"You mean sheep eyes, maybe?"

The guard shrugged. "Yeah I guess so, I'd puke them up too if I ate them, wouldn't you?"

The lady said, "They don't look like sheep eyes to me."

The guard began to break up the crowd, and waved his arms. "OK, OK, enough now." He tried to make light of the situation. "Hey look!" He pointed at an eye and then looked at an old man who was covering his mouth. "That one just winked at you." No one bought into his attempt at humor, so he abandoned his effort and continued. "OK, OK, everyone back away while I have this area cleaned."

McKenzie

Gomez and Apsland stood on a wooden veranda, looking out on an empty residential street. Gomez blew into his hands and then placed them under his armpits. "Damn, hurry up, spring."

Apsland remained quite unanimated in contrast. "Do you intend to wait here all morning?" he inquired.

"This is our main lead, so yes we'll wait," said Gomez. He looked at a picture of the McKenzies.

"A very attractive couple," noted Apsland.

"You know, when I put the cuffs on the bastard who has been doing this…"

Apsland chuckled. "The cuffs." He shook his head. "You won't be able to use cuffs."

Gomez ignored this and continued. "Like you said, I mean look at this couple, they look like they're like movie stars, everything to live for…"

A disheveled, drunk man appeared in the street, staring at Gomez and Apsland. After a few seconds under this man's gaze Gomez grew tired.

"Move along, sir," said Gomez.

The man just clutched his brown paper bag and swayed ever so slightly.

"Sir?" insisted Gomez. "Can you please go about your business?"

The man saluted and began to walk toward them. "Sir?" insisted Gomez, but the man just continued. He took out some keys and walked past Gomez and Apsland. He turned and smiled with perfectly straight, yellow teeth.

Gomez looked at the photograph and then back at this man. "Mr. McKenzie?" said an astonished Gomez.

Mr. McKenzie enjoyed a pause before he responded. "That's right." Mr McKenzie opened the door and walked in, leaving it open.

Gomez inquired if they could enter, but Mr. McKenzie did not respond, he had already found the indentation in his sofa where he passed his life as fast and as far from reality as he could. Gomez looked at Apsland and shrugged his shoulders. They both walked into the house. McKenzie twisted off the top of his bottle. A large bottle with a logo of a cactus wearing a sombrero. Gomez couldn't help thinking, *if you choose to drink yourself to death, why in the hell choose tequila? That's like hanging yourself with barbed wire.*

"Sir, my name is Detective Hector Gomez from Boston South PD, homicide, and this is my associate Mr. Apsland. Do you have a few minutes to spare us? We'd like to…"

Mr. McKenzie thrust his palms against his face. Neither Gomez nor Apsland pressed him: they both knew to allow this man some breathing room.

Mr McKenzie rubbed his eyes and then dropped his hands. He looked up at Gomez with his glazed, red eyes. "If you've come here to tell me my Harriet has been found, then I don't want to hear it." He pointed to the floor. "Found, mutilated, destroyed, I don't want to hear it." He stood up and held the bottle cap in his fist like he was about to pitch a baseball, a tiny, ineffective baseball, posing no threat to anyone. He screamed, "I don't wanna hear it, do you understand?"

Gomez backed away and held up his hands in surrender. "Sir," he said in a calm, clear voice. "We have not found your wife." He raised his eyebrows as if to say, '*Capisce*?

The words registered with Mr. McKenzie. He lowered his hand and slumped back down into the sofa.

"Well, what do you want then?" he asked.

"We're investigating the Life Swapper case. Your wife is the last known person to go missing in the, well the chain, so we wanted to ask you something," said Gomez.

"I told the Italian cop everything over and over again, " said Mr. McKenzie, squinting at Gomez. "What else can I possibly tell you?"

Apsland pointed to a white rectangle on the wall where the painting once hung. "You could tell us what happened to the painting that was there?"

Mr. McKenzie squinted again. "The painting? '*The Hands Resist Him*'?"

"*The Hands Resist Him*?" repeated Gomez.

"Yes, that's what it was called."

"Do you know who the artist was?" asked Gomez.

"Stoneham, W., maybe. You want to know about the painting?"

"Yes, please," said Apsland politely. "It could be most helpful."

Gomez scribbled down the title of the painting and the artist's name in his pad.

When Mr. McKenzie heard the word "helpful," he straightened up and lost his squint. He *did* have hope, it seemed. "I threw it away."

"You threw it away?" repeated Gomez.

"Yes, I hated that thing. Harriet liked it, she loved it, in fact, but I hated it."

"Why?" asked Apsland.

Mr. McKenzie had never spoken about this before. He was aware of this and so considered his words before he spoke. He took a swig from his tequila and grimaced like he had just swallowed acid.

"Because from the moment it arrived, we never had any good luck," he said, staring into the distance.

Apsland pulled him back into the conversation. "Please, go on."

Mr. McKenzie looked back at them both and tried to smile.

"Nothing I could ever put my finger on, just stupid things. I couldn't

sleep, I was sleeping badly, and I don't mean a few nights, I mean I

managed a few hours a night and those hours were more

daydreaming with my eyes closed than anything like real sleeping.

Then our cat, Beans, was killed."

"Your cat?" asked Apsland.

"Yes. At first I thought it must have been some local cruel

bastards. They tortured him, cut him up. I found him when Harriet

was out, and I buried him out there in back of the house. The death

of that cat caused a big argument between Harriet and me."

"How so?" asked Apsland.

"I told her Beans was missing. I couldn't show him to her the

way he was. I put up signs all over the neighborhood, 'Have You

Seen This Cat?' stuff, you know. Even though he was buried out

there, so when she found out that I lied; Jesus."

"But how did she find out?" Gomez asked.

"I'll tell you how, cos he was dug up and placed on our

porch. When she saw him, and then the hole in the ground, she knew

I had buried him." He looked at his bottle. "After what happened to

Harriet, my guess was that the killer of the Johnson girl, the girl that ended up there," he pointed to the floor by his feet, "was the one who took my Harriet. He did it, that's also what the Italian cop thought." He rested his elbows on his knees and began to cry. "That girl, Johnson, her eyes were out."

He placed the bottle over his mouth, not touching his lips and let the tequila pour in, a punishing amount, Gomez and Apsland both physically tensed on seeing it. "It's my fault," he said instantly, explaining this punishment. "It's my fault, I'm her husband I should have protected her." He looked up at the white rectangle on the wall. "Even Beans hated that painting, he used to hiss at it."

"So what did you do with it?" asked Apsland.

"The day after the … events, I got wasted. I hardly ever touched this stuff before, I was a swimmer. I used to model swimwear too, that was my work and Harriet's, that's how we met, a beach shoot for diet 7-Up. Anyway, I got wasted, but I do remember an alley, and an old building, so my guess is I threw it there."

"And where had you bought it?" asked Apsland.

"I didn't, Harriet did, she bought it in town, there are only six or seven shops down there, the gallery is one of them." Mr

McKenzie placed his bottle on the floor and covered his face with his palms again. Apsland sat beside him. He placed his hand on Mr. McKenzie's shoulder and grasped his right wrist.

Mr. McKenzie squeezed his face into his cupped hands. Apsland closed his eyes and began to hum. Almost imperceptible, but he was humming. McKenzie began to roar into his hands. Muffled primeval roars of agony.

This continued for some time. Gomez surprised himself as he became overwhelmed; he turned to a window and looked out into the street, his eyes filling with tears. Never had Gomez been affected so deeply by a stranger's pain. The roaring eventually began to fade.

Gomez was angry at himself, he felt impotent, useless. He turned to Mr. McKenzie and etched out words in granite. "Mr. McKenzie, I promise I'll do everything I can to get your wife back."

Mr. McKenzie dropped his hands from his wet face and looked at Gomez, a battle of hope against despair raged on his face. Apsland also looked at Gomez, but disparagingly.

"Do you have any questions for us?" asked Gomez.

"Yes, why did you ask me about the painting?"

"There's a chance that in some way that painting, either through ownership or in some other way, is a factor in the Life Swapper case"

"A factor?" repeated Mr. McKenzie.

"Yes, that's all I can really say for the moment, but you'll be the first to know if it turns up anything."

"You know I always did wonder about that," said Mr. McKenzie.

"About what?" said Gomez.

"The eyes, that doll in the painting had no eyes."

*

Back out into the cold morning air, Gomez turned to Apsland and asked, "What did you do in there?"

Apsland did not respond. Instead he snapped at Gomez. "Why did you tell him you'd try to get his wife back?"

"What?" said Gomez. "Why shouldn't I say that?"

"You shouldn't make promises you can't keep," said Apsland, making his annoyance known in his harsh footsteps.

"I only promised I'd try. Anyway, how do you know I can't get his wife back?

"Because," Apsland stopped just as they reached Gomez's car, "she is no longer alive, that's why!"

"How do you know she's dead?" pushed an equally annoyed Gomez.

"I never said she was dead," said Apsland.

Tea Time With The Dolls

Olivia sat on her side of her room on her large Aladdin rug. Patricia leaned on the door's frame with her arms folded as she stood half in the room and half on the landing. Olivia had her back to the door, but she knew her mother was watching her. She placed a large teddy bear at the small table, where he sat towering above three Barbie dolls, their plastic faces unable to show any discomfort or alarm at having tea with a huge bear. As Patricia studied the guests, she couldn't help laughing to herself that it'd be the same in reality, the glamorous female guests would still be unable to show any emotion at having a bear at the table, the Botox would see to that.

Poor Spider Man sat emasculated, forced to drink tea from rose-pink cups.

"Did George say it was OK?" asked Patricia. "You remember how annoyed he was last time, don't you?"

"That was different, Mommy. He was annoyed cos I put the Hulk in a carriage, and George said the Hulk's not a baby."

"OK, honey," smiled Patricia. She caressed Olivia's fine blonde, almost white hair. "I have to go downstairs now."

"Oh Mommy, can't you stay here for a few minutes?"

"I can't, honey, I have things to do. I'll be back up as soon as I'm done, how's that?"

Olivia nodded with the cuteness that only preschoolers have.

Patricia's heart soared. Looking down on that perfect little human, a flush of wonder swept over her.

There she stood, the proud mother, sending beams of love from her heart down to her child, wearing the best of smiles, the smile of a mother's love. However, what Patricia was not aware of, what she could not have been aware of, was that she was not the only one staring at Olivia. Standing to Patricia's left was the boy from the painting, to her right was the doll, so close they were almost touching Patricia's hips. Patricia continued to send heart beams down at Olivia. The boy looked at Olivia with a frozen snarl, his mouth partially open and his head tilted down, his black eyes contrasting against his thin bleached skin. The doll, enigmatic and devious, waited with evil intention, her empty, eyeless sockets darker and deeper than two bottomless wells.

If only Patricia could see them. "OK, honey, back soon."

Patricia disappeared down the stairs. Olivia gave her dolls voices. Apparently Spider Man drank more tea than anyone else at the table. "More tea, Mr. Spider Man?"

"Yes, please."

Olivia turned around sharply, pouring invisible tea all over the small table. She stood up and looked out through her open doorway into the landing. "Mommy, is that you?" She placed the small pink teapot down on the table.

She peered out into the landing. Behind her, in her room, stood the boy and the doll.

"George? Is that you?"

She stood in the landing, not really knowing why. She turned and walked back into her room.

The sound of Olivia's scream instantly ceased three activities. George threw his drawing on the floor, Daniel's laptop landed on the floor as it fell off his legs, and Patricia literally threw an unwashed pot in the sink.

In an instant, all three were in the room with Olivia. Olivia was sniffling and holding her doll, Alice.

"What's wrong, honey?" said Daniel.

Olivia clutched Alice into her chest.

"Honey?" persisted Daniel gently.

Olivia looked up at them. She took Alice from her clutches and held her up to the suspended gaze of the family. Olivia screamed, "She's got no eyes! Her eyes have been pulled off"

Patricia picked up both Olivia and Alice and wrapped herself around them. "Oh my God, honey." Olivia's sniffling was over, now it was total bawling. She pressed her face into Patricia's shoulder and cried. Patricia tried to absorb her pain.

Daniel looked at the small plastic table. He turned to George accusingly.

George, horrified at the mere suggestion, shook his head adamantly.

Daniel's expression turned aggressive. "Did you do this? Did you do this to your sister?"

"No, no!" screamed George.

"Just because she took Spider Man, did you do this?" shouted Daniel. Patricia put Olivia down and turned to Daniel, enraged. Daniel looked at her. He was so convinced of his ludicrous accusation he automatically believed Patricia's outrage was also with George.

George didn't answer, he ran off in tears. Daniel began to chase after him but Patricia grabbed his sleeve and yanked him back violently.

"What?" she screamed. "Have you gone insane? You accuse *our son* of this? *Our son?*"

Daniel was wide-eyed and had no response. He just breathed heavily. But Patricia hadn't finished. She pulled Daniel toward the painting. "That's who did it, that's who did it."

Daniel stared blankly at the painting, his face pale. He was distant, confused.

Patricia began to cry. "Can't you see? It's them."

Daniel squeezed his head between his arms, clasping his fingers together behind his neck as if fighting some great dilemma.

Patricia squinted at him as she tried to understand upon what basis he had any doubt. "What's wrong with you? Why are you so torn? What is there to think about? We have to get rid of it, Daniel!" cried Patricia through streaming tears.

Daniel snapped. "Get rid of it? I paid fifteen hundred dollars for it."

Daniel's attitude was so complete in its utter contrast to logic, it made Patricia physically step backwards.

"And you're surprised, I ask? My God, Daniel, you accuse *our son* of something you know he'd never do, something you normally wouldn't accuse him of in a million years and you are surprised? You've changed, Daniel, you've changed, that thing has made you change."

"Mommy," said Olivia. After a pause she continued "I don't want Daddy to change."

"Neither do I, honey," replied Patricia. "Neither do I."

Daniel turned to Patricia. "OK." He turned back to the painting. "I'll get rid of it."

"When?" asked Patricia quickly and distrustfully.

Daniel looked at Patricia in outrage. He had the audacity to be offended by this distrust, or possibly he was faking his offense, either way it was infuriating. But Patricia said nothing. He was getting rid of the painting and she didn't want to risk derailing that. He pulled it off the wall and headed down the stairs.

As soon as the door slammed, George ran upstairs to his mother, and they sat on the floor and consoled each other. The sound of Daniel's car driving further and further away made Patricia cry again. "What's wrong, Mommy?" asked Olivia.

"Nothing, sweetheart, everything's gonna be fine now, fine."

Looking for Urska

Mateusz sat in his van. Spread out on the dashboard was a large printout of *The Hands Resist Him*, next to which sat a map covered in blue and black dots, more black than blue. He took a black felt marker and drew over a blue spot.

"Amaze Gallery, no, no good, no one knows, no one knows." His head fell back against the headrest as he squeezed his eyes tightly shut and rubbed them with two ink-smudged black and blue fingers.

"Why don't you call me, Urska? Call me."

He looked at his phone. It immediately began to ring; he flinched and dropped the black marker.

"Hello?"

"Hello," responded an official-sounding voice. "Mr. Boruch?"

"Yes, yes, this is Mr. Boruch."

"Good afternoon, Sir, this is Litchfield County Sheriff's office"

"Yes, yes, please tell me? You have found Urska?"

"No sir, but she has been seen, she was last seen at a bus station in New Milford, she was heading to Binghamton."

"Binghamton? I have never heard of it."

"Oh," said the voice, sounding disappointed. "We were hoping you'd know who she'd want to see there, or why she was headed there?"

"No idea," said Mateusz, as he marked Binghamton on the map in blue.

"Please be sure to call us immediately if she contacts you, OK?"

"Sure," responded an invigorated Mateusz. "Sure, I will."

"Sir, it's a criminal offense if you are in possession of information of a fugitive's whereabouts and do not advise us." The voice paused. "Do you understand?"

"Yes sir, I do understand. I honestly do not know why she is there. I am sitting here looking at my phone hoping she will call; in fact, I hoped your call was her calling."

"OK, sir, have a good day."

"Thank you, and you too, thank you."

Mateusz hung up and managed to smile. The smile came with glassy eyes but was nevertheless a smile. "Fugitive." He chuckled sadly. "My little Urska."

The Gallery

Ernst Pfeiffer stood between Gomez and Apsland. "*The Hands Resist Him?* What would the police want with that?" He smiled enigmatically, suggesting some knowledge of the painting.

"We have an ongoing investigation and the painting has been something that has popped up along the way." Gomez shrugged away any importance. "In this line of work we have to rule things in or out, no matter how unlikely."

Ernst Pfeiffer continued to smile mischievously. "Hm, a likely story." He placed his left hand on his hip and gently checked his hair parting, making sure it was immaculate.

Gomez turned to Apsland. "Can you believe this guy?"

"OK sir," said Gomez forcefully. "You win, it'll make or break the case, and if it does you'll be a star and when they make a movie about it, I'll make sure John Malkovich plays you, how's that?"

Ernst Pfeiffer looked at Apsland and placed his hand over his mouth, feigning outrage. "Wow, Mr. Apsland," he said in a stage whisper. "Is he always so touchy?" He looked back at Gomez and sneered jovially. "Anyway, Malkovich will be fine, it's a deal."

"My knowledge of the painting," he continued, "is probably limited. It might be that you know more than I do regarding this unusual work of William Stoneham."

"William," exclaimed Gomez as he wrote it down in his notepad.

"Ah," said a content Ernst Pfieffer. "Maybe I do know more than you."

"Where did you get it?" Gomez asked.

"I bought it from within the trade, as a lot of, I think, around twenty paintings and a few sculptures."

"Do you know anything about Stoneham?" Gomez asked.

"A little, to understand Stoneham, you have to go back to 1972 and Binghamton."

The Gas Station

Mateusz turned on his headlights. The winter sun had kept him company as it sat directly ahead on the freeway, divided on either side by the forest, but finally it disappeared behind the trees to the west, this was to the right for Mateusz.

"Welcome to Binghamton."

Mateusz had read that sign at least ten miles back and there was nothing yet, no sign of Binghamton. *Why welcome me and then not be there?* He had passed many junctions and thin dirt side roads that went somewhere off into the forest to the left or right.

Anyway here was a gas station. He originally had no intention of stopping, but that was when he thought Binghamton would have shown itself, so he wouldn't have needed nor wanted to stop. He rolled into the gas station, he still had a quarter tank of gas, but he pulled in nevertheless.

He got out and stretched. The garage was covered in rusting metal signs for products that no longer existed. 'Ease the freeze with FREOL' 'A winner on wings, Winguard wing mirrors' There was also a Le Mans advert from the early 1920's. Mateusz couldn't help wondering how much these items were worth.

"Yeah," said an old man, then he turned his back to Mateusz and pointed over his shoulder with his thumb. "Winguard." His blue overall had the same name and slogan. He laughed. "I've still got a pair if you're interested?"

"Of the mirrors?" Mateusz said, and smiled

"Yes, sure, they come with a free Ford Super Deluxe 1947, it's out back full of tires." He laughed and rubbed his hands with a dirty cloth.

"Where are you headed?"

"Binghamton."

"You want me to wash your windshield?"

"Sure, yes please."

The old man picked up a bucket of water and walked around to the front of Mateusz's van. He cleaned the windshield with a squeegee.

"Binghamton," said the old man. "It's just up the way."

"OK, I was worried I went past it."

"Not a chance, it's pretty big you know."

"Oh yes?"

"Yeah, we have a bowling alley, a museum, a library, our own fire department, police department, we don't need to share anything. I say that, but I know we've made arrests and put out fires for some of our neighbors, so we share, but 'to' people, if you get what I mean, we don't need any help."

The old man looked down into the van. "*The Hands Resist Him*! What are you doing with that?"

Mateusz was stunned. "You know this painting?"

The old man put down the bucket. "Of course I do." He took out his rag and wiped his hands again. "Everyone around here knows about William Stoneham."

"William!" whispered Mateusz to himself. He continued. "Why everyone around here?"

"Because he lives here."

Mateusz's eyes lit up. "He lives here?"

"That's right, and he has since 1972."

McCabe's Report

"In 1972 a young artist named William Stoneham, resident of California, was arrested for murder and sent to Binghamton Asylum."

"And this is the artist who painted this painting?" asked O'Hara.

"Yes, sir."

"As per your instructions, Captain," said Marvin, "we checked all the residences. And all of them, that is, the ones where we could get to speak to someone, in some way or the other came into contact with that painting."

O'Hara looked at a large blow-up of the painting "So it looks like Gomez is on to something."

"We were kinda disappointed when we heard Stoneham was at Binghamton, he's still there to this day."

"Disappointed?" quizzed O'Hara. "Why?"

"Ah we hoped maybe the artist was a nut and stalked people who bought his painting, popped out their eyes and stuff."

"I see," said O'Hara. "That would'a made sense." He paused. "An admirer, maybe? An accomplice? Or someone he worked with?"

"Well," said Marvin. "We're still open on the admirer and accomplice angle, but the someone he worked with was the someone he murdered."

"Oh? Tell me?"

McCabe looked at his notes. "Abigail Kinsella."

"He murdered her?"

"That's right, Captain, right there in his California studio."

"Why? How?" asked O'Hara.

The Gallery

"He twisted her head off," said Ernst Pfeiffer.

"Holy shit." Gomez said. "Twisted her head off?"

"I thought you cops had heard it all," said Ernst Pfeiffer, making air quotes.

"So did I," responded Gomez.

"He told the arresting police officer it only took four twists, I would have thought more, wouldn't you?" asked Ernst Pfeiffer.

Gomez hesitated, irritated at having to use his brain to consider this. *Stick to the subject for Christ's sake*, he thought. "I guess so, go on."

"From that very day, he was sent to the Binghamton insane asylum."

"Do you know if he's still there?" asked Gomez.

"I have heard nothing to the contrary, at the time he claimed he was innocent."

"Did you mention any of this to the McKenzies before they bought the painting?" asked Apsland.

Ernst Pfeiffer smiled disingenuously. "I didn't think it was important."

The Gas Station

The old garage attendant pointed through the windshield. "He said it was that painting that murdered his assistant, at his trial his lawyer pleaded insanity. Stoneham, from what I know has always protested his innocent, through all these almost thirty years, he has never even been at a parole hearing as he won't admit it, and they say, if he won't admit it then there's no chance for release."

"Do you think he did it?" asked Mateusz.

"I don't know, but what I do know is that a painting can't twist someone's head off."

"Where is the asylum?" Mateusz asked soberly.

"It's back a-ways," the old man said, looking in the air at his mental map. "Going back it'd be on your left, a small road, sign posted, New York State Inebriate Asylum." The old garage attendant placed the nozzle of the pump in the van, he clicked the trigger into a lock position which left the pump to continue on its own, leaving his hands free. Only to fold them as they then had nothing to do.

"'Inebriate'? Doesn't that mean drunks?"

"Yes, they treated alcoholics there, they saw it as a mental illness, anyway drunks, murderers and everything in-between."

"OK, thanks."

"You're gonna go there? What for?" the old man pulled out the pump nozzle.

"Um, I wanted to interview Mr. Stoneham, that's why I'm here."

The old man chuckled. "But you didn't know he was in the asylum until I just told you, or why he was there."

"No, no, so thanks." Mateusz thought on his feet, or lied on his feet. "I knew he was here, I just didn't know where, I was just interested in the painting, I didn't know all of this story."

The old man didn't believe a word of it, but equally he didn't care either way. "I'm not sure of the opening hours." The gas pump chimed. He pulled out the nozzle and looked around at the pump. "Twenty-two dollars, please."

Mateusz unfolded some crumpled bills.

"Ah," said the old garage attendant. "I just remembered, part of it is derelict, so remember that, otherwise you'll think it's closed.

They applied for a grant to fix it, a whole side of the complex is too dangerous to enter."

The Gallery

"Do you have a computer with an internet connection?" Gomez asked.

"I have a computer, but no access to the World Wide Web, I'm afraid," responded Ernst Pfeiffer.

Gomez pressed a contact on his cell phone and placed the phone to his ear whilst still speaking to Ernst Pfeiffer. "Is there anyone in town who does?"

"There's the Oxford hotel, turn left out of here, then first left and it's halfway up the hill on the right, they have access."

"OK, thanks." He looked at his phone and ended the call. "The line's busy."

The Precinct

"It's going straight to voicemail," said O'Hara. "Shall I leave a message?"

"Yeah," said Marvin. "It can't hurt."

The Gallery

Gomez and Apsland marched down the quiet street as directed. Up on the hill on the right, just where it was supposed to be, was the Oxford Hotel. A beautiful old building painted in white with black wood accents. An affront to this authentic beauty was the adornment of credit card stickers plastered all over the delicate original glass.

"What do you want to search? The address of the asylum?" asked Apsland as he held the door for Gomez.

"Well, yeah, that too, but now we know the name of the artist and the title of the work, so now we, what is it they say? 'Google.' Stoneham can wait, he's not going anywhere. We need to find out where the painting is now."

Gomez and Apsland leaned on the front desk in identical postures, one elbow on the counter, one hand in a pocket and one leg placed behind the other; they were a horizontal flip of each other. Gomez broke up the symmetry when he pinged the bell.

A teenage boy arrived with a center part in his hair and a waxed pencil moustache, a black bow tie, white stiff short and a black waist coat, grey troausers with a shiny grey stipe on the sides (*I don't wanna work for my uncle. There's nothing else, you'll work for your uncle.*)

"May I help you?" asked the teenager.

Gomez showed the boy his badge. "Do you have a computer with access to the internet that we can use? Police business."

"Yes, sir we do," he responded clearly. The boy had no natural 'in' for an explanation of why he was dressed the way he was. God knows he tried to work one in every time he was embarrassed, which was every time someone came to the hotel, that is, apart from really old people or very young children, they didn't need an explanation, he didn't feel the same need to supply one. Whichever it was, the teenager usually did just fine, at least he always made it clear it wasn't his idea. His embarrassment, intentionally visible, took care of that.

He led them to an office in the back. Gomez sat down with Apsland standing to his right. The teenager remained, twisting his moustache.

"Nice stache," said Gomez.

The teenager had his in. "It's my uncle, he owns this place, he's big on authenticity, so he insists I dress, we dress like, authentic-like." His face relaxed, ah the liberation.

"Shame he doesn't extend that attention to detail as far as the door with the credit card stickers," observed Apsland.

"Yes," agreed the teenager. "Ye Olde Credit Card Door."

Gomez and Apsland smiled but they did not continue or encourage the conversation, they had work to do. The teenager understood and shifted into action. "Oh, uh, yes, please excuse me, if you need anything, just yell."

Gomez immediately turned in his chair and began tapping away. He started with the painting's title, *The Hands Resist Him.*

He got to the *R* and there it was.

"eBay?" said Gomez. He clicked.

The expired eBay listing appeared on the screen, unveiling the boy and the doll as the pixels loaded. "Jesus, it's been on eBay."

Gomez read through the text: "When we received this painting, we thought it was really good art. The person we bought it from found it abandoned in an old brewery." Gomez turned to

Apsland. "So that's probably where McKenzie dumped it." He continued. "At the time we wondered why a seemingly perfectly fine painting would be discarded like that.

Today we don't. One morning our four-and-a-half-year-old daughter claimed that the children in the picture were fighting, and coming into her room during the night. Now, I don't believe in UFOs or Elvis being alive but my husband was alarmed.

To my amusement, he set up a motion-triggered camera for three nights. After three nights there were pictures. The last two pictures shown are from that stakeout. After seeing the boy seemingly exiting the painting as though he was being threatened, we decided the painting has to go. Please judge for yourself. Before you do, please read the following warning and disclaimer. "Warning! Do not bid on this painting if you are susceptible to stress-related diseases, faint of heart, or are unfamiliar with supernatural events. By bidding on this painting, you agree to release the owners of all liability in relation to the sale or any events happening after the sale that might be contributed to this painting. This painting may or may not possess supernatural powers that could impact or change your life. However, by bidding, you agree to exclusively bid on the value of the artwork, disregarding to the last two photos featured in this auction. You agree not to hold the previous owners responsible for any untoward events that may occur after purchase."

The Precinct

"'One question to you eBayers,'" read O'Hara. "Listen to this." He looked at an equally entertained McCabe and Marvin, they didn't respond, not wanting to delay their further entertainment. He continued, "'We want our house to be blessed after the painting is gone, does anybody know who is qualified to do that? The size of the painting…' blah, blah, blah. 'As I have had several questions, here the following answers. There was no odor left behind in the room. There were no voices, or the smell of gunpowder, not footprints or strange fluids on the wall. To deter questions of this sort, there are no ghosts in the world, no supernatural powers. This is just a painting, and most of these things…' that's what it says '…most of these things have an explanation. In this case, it was probably a fluke effect of light. I encourage you to bid on the artwork, and consider the last two photographs as pure entertainment.' Yeah I'd agree with that. '…and please do not take them into consideration when bidding. As we think it is a good idea to bless any house, we still welcome input into that procedure.

"'This auction is nearing the end. I want to thank the more than thirteen thousand people who took the time to look at this image on eBay. I appreciate the more than thirty suggestions that I received regarding blessing the house, exorcising and cleansing. Seven emails reported strange or irregular events taking place when viewing this image. And I will relay two suggestions made by the senders. First, not to use this image as the background on a computer screen, and second, not to display this image around animals or children. Last but not least, thanks for appreciating the art as well.'"

"Look, Captain," said McCabe. "It sold on February the twelfth."

The Oxford Hotel

"That's less than a few weeks ago," said Apsland.

"Leydenx4 is the winner but there's no address," said Gomez.

He took out his cell phone and pressed redial. He scrolled through the listing on the computer, looking at the images of the boy and doll as he held his phone to his ear.

O'Hara answered. "Gomez?"

"Yeah, Captain, it's me."

"Daniel Leyden, 46 Lakeside Drive, Manchester, New Hampshire, they're a family of four," said O'Hara without explanation.

"Wow," said Gomez. "You know, you're not half bad."

"OK Gomez," said O'Hara "You've done great, so far the two Ps have served you well."

"All we need now is some Pluck," said Gomez.

"OK," said O'Hara. "We don't want any more victims. So how's your 'I'm a civilian who'd really like to buy your painting' act?"

"It's superb," said Gomez.

"What car are you in? Marked or unmarked?"

"Unmarked."

"Good."

"How much should I offer?"

"It went for fifteen hundred dollars, so double? But the fact is we need that painting, so when the perp strikes again I want the owner to be one of us in a secure trap house. So give him what he asks for."

"Should I visit them tonight? It'll be around eight by the time we get there."

"No, speak to them tomorrow, but make a pass-by tonight, just to see the lay of the land."

"Sure thing, we're on our way."

Urska's Bus

Urska sat at the back of the bus above the engine, just right of center on the long seat. This bus, the third, would take her directly to Binghamton Asylum. One very long very narrow road. 'I don't even need to turn a corner,' as the bus driver had put it. The vibrations of the engine rumbled through Urska's frail body.

She looked down the aisle of the empty bus out through the window as the bus made its way down the dark road. The trees on either side seemed to turn and look at her as she passed. The headlights of the bus revealed the thin gray trees, one after the other, like dead Revolutionary soldiers who had walked down to the road to see what was going on.

The darkness outside was balanced out by the internal lights of the bus. Instead of looking *out* the windows Urska was looking *at* the windows, their black reflection forcing her to look inside the bus. She concentrated ahead at the road. The road surface became bumpy. Urska grabbed the backrest of the seat in front of her. She didn't say anything, in fact she was only too happy to get to Stoneham as soon as she could, as fast she could take, but it was getting reckless. They hit one bump so hard, she physically left her seat. Urska broke her self-imposed decorum.

"Can you slow down, please?"

There was no response. Again, a small bump, a small bump multiplied by speed, multiplied by poor suspension and again Urska leaped from her seat. She yelled, "Can you slow down, please?"

The driver ignored her. The bus continued to rivet down the lane. Urska clung on as she leaped again from her seat. "Hey!" she screamed. "Slow down!" She was holding on like a rodeo star. They were going to crash, Urska knew it. She tried to unclasp her hands from the seat, but they were fixed tight. In the reflection kneeling on the seat in front of her was the boy, his dead corpse refusing to be still, his tiny white hands clasped over hers. He dug his small nails in as he grimaced in mocking sorrow.

The doll sat next to Urska. The doll leaned her head against her, instantly turning the left side of Urska's body cold.

Urska screamed to the driver. "Slow down, stop the bus!"

The driver's head turned 180 degrees back towards Urska, the crunching of his spine audible through the roar of the engine. He smiled at Urska. "You want me to slow down, lady?" he said, his hands gripping the wheel.

Urska layered screams upon screams, this final layer was her last, she had no more terror to give; she had reached the ceiling of her torment. Urska wanted to be free, this moment must end. The large gray tree that they were headed toward was a most welcome sight. Although only mere seconds until her death, she willed the tree closer. At seventy miles per hour, her wish was quickly granted. The bus smashed straight into the tree, smashing the cab in two. As Urska flew through the air, she realized she was not hitting anything, and she wasn't dead yet, there was just a whizzing sound as she flew past branches. *I can still die, I will hit something*, she thought.

She landed in a bed of leaves and bramble, sitting upright. *I didn't hit anything!* The will to live was back, instantly, like a trick candle that you can't blow out.

She stood up and made her way back to the burning bus. The windshield was gone. So was the driver. Urska traced the trajectory of his possible route. Sure enough, there he lay, about the same distance as Urska had flown.

Urska ran back to the road.

"Help," she heard.

She stopped and stood perfectly still. Again, she heard: "Help." She turned.

The driver raised his hand from his bed of leaves. He began to stand, his body facing the opposite direction of his head. The leaves fell off his back, where his chest should have been. He was looking at Urska. "Lady, what happened?" he asked.

"Oh Jesus," said Urska. "Please sit down."

The driver started to walk toward her. "What's wrong?" he asked.

"No, no, sit down, you are injured."

"What's wrong?" he insisted.

Urska's mind spun. *What is this now? It's just a diabolical game of trick or treat.*

Trick, thought Urska. "Fuck you." She walked backwards, the driver smiled deviously, he also walked backwards, but facing her. She turned and ran back out onto the road.

Alice

Daniel was back home. He leaned in the doorway of Olivia's room. *Physical evidence*, thought Daniel. Olivia's doll had no eyes. He contented himself with this idea: e*vidence means it could have been George as easily as this fantasy ghost nonsense.*

He walked into Olivia's room and sat down at the abandoned tea party. He picked up Alice and traced her eye sockets. He ran his hand around over the carpet, searching for the missing eyes.

To his left in the landing something shot past his vision. He placed Alice back down on the carpet and got up slowly, he peered out onto the landing. He heard a sniffling coming from his room.

As he entered, he saw it was Olivia, sitting on his bed. He sat down next to her and began to stroke her hair.

"Daddy?"

"Yes, honey?"

"You're not gonna change, are you?"

"No sweetheart, Daddy's not gonna change."

Olivia's smile won over her sniffling. She turned and hugged Daniel, who continued to stroke her hair. They sat in silence, consoling each other.

Daniel ran his fingers through her long fine hair, he gently ran his hand over her tiny soft back, stroking her, each stroke released warm signals of affection. Daniel began to relax he partially closed his eyes and released himself into this magic. He sat like a cat purring. He continued to run his fingers up and down her back. Suddenly his expression changed, his fingers stopped. Her back was solid, cold and bony. He grabbed her small arms and pushed her from their embrace, he leaped up and backwards from the bed.

Staring back at him was not his Olivia, but the doll from the painting. Daniel gasped aloud. "Jesus, Jesus!"

The nonsense that he had been dismissing now sat on his bed, in the middle of his bed, completely unaided. He turned to the doorway and shouted, "Olivia, George!" he screamed, "Patricia, where are the kids?"

The children heard the commotion and came running into his room. Daniel fell to his knees and embraced them both. His whole body trembled.

"What happened, Daddy?" asked George in concern.

Daniel turned to look at the doll but it was gone.

"Daddy, you're trembling," said Olivia.

"Dad! What happened?" insisted George.

Daniel could barely speak, he was too close to tears. He just shook his head and managed to squeeze out the word "Nothing."

From downstairs, Patricia shouted, "Daniel, did you call me?"

Daniel took a breath. "It's OK, forget it, I wanted to know where the kids were, but it's OK, they're up here with me."

"Daniel," said Patricia from downstairs. "The kids are down here with me."

From within their cold embrace, the two figures that tightly held Daniel began to snigger. They slowly began to release their arms. Daniel's adrenaline sent his heart thumping against his chest, but his limbs were beyond his control.

The faces of the boy and the doll came into view. At that exact moment, the door slammed shut and the lights went out simultaneously.

Patricia could hear Daniel screaming.

She thrust herself up the stairs. She leaped to the door, slamming her whole body weight against it, but it would not open.

She banged on the door. "Daniel! Daniel!"

She kicked and punched the door. She stood backwards and prepared herself for a final charge at the door. Daniel's screaming stopped, and the door quietly clicked open.

The children arrived behind Patricia. They all entered the room. Daniel was on his knees staring blankly ahead. He looked at his family and cupped his face in his hands.

Mateusz. The Road to Binghamton

There it was, a rusted metal sign with buckshot dents, hidden behind some twigs like old thin fingers covering a guilty face. "New York State Inebriate Asylum."

Mateusz untwisted his spot lamp and began to drive down the narrow road. He rolled both windows down halfway. He wanted to make sure he had every chance of finding Urska even if that meant he would be cold.

The cold air rattled into the back of his van, vibrating the steel side panels. Both he and the van were shaking. The same gray twisted trees stood at the foot of the road peering into the cab like fans of a bicycle race who encroached too near the cyclists. Mateusz was moving his head from left to right to straight ahead, just in case he should see Urska. The rear-view mirror revealed nothing more than a wall of fog directly behind his van, closing a door behind him as he passed on deeper and deeper toward the asylum, a door he would have preferred remained open, even just a little.

The narrow road was hypnotizing, mile after mile of endless straight road. Only the occasional dip, or gradient to remind him it was not a dream.

Breaking this monotony was something yellow blinking in the fog. The blinking grew nearer. As he got nearer, the blinking was revealed to be the rear hazard lights of a mangled wreck. Mateusz pulled up beside the crumpled bus. Still poised in its deadly head butt against the victorious tree.

He cautiously got out of his van and then ran inside the bus, searching up and down the aisle and looking under seats. He ran outside chasing around the perimeter of the bus, but there was no one. Just the smell of gasoline.

He reached into his pocket for his cell phone to call the emergency services. Its display lit only to read zero connection.

He turned sharply and got back in his van. He started the engine and crept along as quietly as his engine would allow. He hadn't driven far when he noticed a shape, after miles of trees Mateusz could instantly spot an anomaly. To the left at the bottom of a decline, slumped against a tree, Mateusz thought he could see the outline of a person.

He switched off his engine and rolled along in neutral, coming to a halt with the squeaking of his brakes. He switched on his flashlight and pointed it toward the tree.

He gulped. This really was an anomaly. It wasn't simply that the man's head was facing the other way. It was the distance from the crash. *How did he get here? No one can survive that injury. Is it possible?*

He climbed out of his van and walked toward the victim. He inadvertently walked in front of his headlights, casting the body into shadow, and then he moved immediately.

He walked around, circling the man at a comfortable distance. The man's blue uniform suggested to Mateusz that he was the driver. His face pressed against the tree. Mateusz asked calmly, "How the hell did you get all the way…" and then after a pause, the pause being a tribute to logic, a dedication to reason, he screamed, "here?"

Mateusz leaned back and flicked his foot at the driver's foot. After this pitiful test, he cautiously crept nearer to this twisted abomination. He reached down and tried to feel for a pulse on the driver's wrist. "Well, however you did get here, you're dead now."

Mateusz walked backwards to his van and climbed in. He glanced down at his map. There was still a long way to go to reach the asylum. *Maybe she's OK, maybe she was picked up? What picked her up, there are no cars on this lost road, she's out there.*

Mateusz looked up, as there was something large in his peripheral vision, something that had not been there before. He turned to his left. The driver was standing next to the tree, staring at Mateusz.

Mateusz screamed. The driver began to walk backwards toward Mateusz. Mateusz turned on the ignition, but it was dead. "What?" he screamed. All of those movies he laughed at were now laughing at him. He could hear the driver's feet swishing through the dead leaves.

Mateusz kept turning the key in quick succession but it was completely dead. He looked back out the open window; the driver was now only a few yards away. Mateusz remembered that he had rolled down the hill, and the van was in neutral. He immediately put the shifter back into park and turned the ignition, whoosh, and instant take off. Mateusz sped away and then after five seconds at forty miles per hour, he screeched to a halt, remaining parked at a diagonal across the road. He looked back out of the window toward the driver who had collapsed to his knees, falling forwards onto the back of his head.

Mateusz jumped out of the cab and placed his hands on his knees. He was preparing to be sick, but the moment passed. He just spat and rubbed his face, and then he ran his hands through his hair, hard. This ritual seemed to help keep him from surrendering to his fear. He looked back at the collapsed body. "Oh shit, maybe he *was* alive?" *I should have tried to help him instead of running away. But you did try, you checked his pulse. Yes, but maybe I was wrong. Yes, could be. I have been terrible, I should have checked. I am terrible, scared, a pussy, that is what Americans would call my behavior, or Robert, the English guy, he would call me a wanker. Then it's not too late, he could easily still be alive, why don't you go back and check now, then?*

"No! No, sorry, sorry," he climbed back in his van. "No, no, this is all connected, he's dead, he's dead, fuck you! No one can live and have their neck broken like that, *you're* a pussy! *you're* a wanker for being so naïve. Yeah 'go back, go back' and then what? Fuck you!"

The Refrigerator

It was decided that that night, they would all sleep together. The children were supposed to go to bed first at their normal time of eight o'clock, and give Daniel and Patricia a chance to talk. However, they fell asleep too on either side of the children. Olivia was in a deep wonderland, both hands squashed under her cheek. George, on the other hand, was wide awake. Not because of the day's stresses, but simply because he needed to pee, and Daniel's arm was lying against his chest.

Like a limbo dancer, George slowly wormed his way down the bed. He turned his face so as not to have to confront Daniel's heavy arm with his nose. Then he was out.

He walked out into the landing past his and Olivia's room, toward the bathroom. He crept along, as he didn't want to wake anyone up. His dad hadn't been specific tonight when he said, "We'll all sleep together," he didn't stress what to do for toilet breaks, was it OK to break the sleep together rule if you needed to take toilet trip? George had already answered this.

He now had a dilemma. *Do I flush?*

If he flushed, he risked waking the family and getting nagged. If he didn't, he risked them seeing the un-flushed toilet in the morning and getting nagged.

Ah, but George was clever. He took a small basin and filled it with water, he put the tap on gentle and tilted the basin underneath the tap. The skill involved suggested George could probably pour a good beer. He carefully poured the water into the toilet bowl. A good result, but not perfect, so he filled it once more, and this did the trick. The water was pure and clear and no one would be the wiser.

He made his way back to the bedroom. A light shone up from downstairs. It wasn't there before. Maybe someone had gotten up for a little snack? Then George thought of a little snack. *Yum.*

He snuck downstairs and walked into the dining room. Over to his right in the open plan kitchen, he could see that the refrigerator door was wide open.

He walked toward it to close it. Only as he got closer did he start to add some things up. What had happened a few hours earlier, why had Dad insisted they sleep together? Olivia's doll. Why was this light not on before? And no one was down here. He stood in front of the refrigerator, staring at it for an explanation. The refrigerator couldn't oblige, but there was an explanation, standing behind him. George suddenly felt this presence. His eyes widened and he looked to his left with his eyes without turning his head, then in one quick movement he turned. As he did so, the refrigerator door slammed shut, sending him into blackness.

*

"George?" said Daniel loudly as he bolted upright in bed.

Patricia opened her eyes. In an instant, she was completely awake. She threw off the blankets like a Spanish toreador and rushed for the door. She stood at the entrance to the landing. "George!" she screamed.

Daniel ran past her and into the bathroom. Olivia began to cry. Patricia ran back into the room and grabbed Olivia.

Daniel ran downstairs and into the dining room, screaming George's name. Patricia, with Olivia in her arms, made her way to the bottom of the stairs, screaming even louder as Olivia covered her ears.

"Maybe he went outside?" asked Patricia, but she had such little belief in this possibility that she barely finished the sentence.

Daniel answered, "No, the alarms would have gone off. I'm calling the police." He ran for the phone, still screaming George's name.

Patricia handed Olivia to Daniel. "I'll search the laundry room." She sprinted down the small steps and ran into the laundry room. It was empty. She turned to her right and noticed that the internal garage door was open.

"Daniel, did you leave the garage door open?"

"No, I parked outside tonight."

"Outside?"

Patricia walked toward the open garage door.

At that moment, there was a loud, urgent knocking on the door simultaneous with the doorbell being rung non-stop. Before Daniel could react, he heard the words, "Police, open up."

He opened the door, Detective Gomez stood on the porch, holding up his identification. Next to him stood a concerned Dyson Von Bilbow Apsland.

"Sir, we heard the commotion, my name is Detective Hector Gomez of Boston South PD, this is—"

Gomez was interrupted by a chilling scream that came from the garage. Daniel immediately turned and ran toward the stairs; he was closely followed by Apsland and Gomez, who had drawn his revolver.

Patricia was standing, looking into the garage. Lying there in at the back of the dark, empty garage was a body. Gomez and Apsland pushed past and looked over at the body and then at each other. Daniel peered over the three sets of shoulders. On seeing the body, he screamed, "George, George!"

At that moment, Patricia attempted to rush into the room. Gomez grabbed her and wrestled her back. She fought against him, screaming her son's name. Daniel put his daughter down and tried to push past Apsland. Apsland grabbed Daniel's arms and shouted firmly, "No! No!"

Daniel shouted his son's name over Apsland's shoulder. Olivia was screaming.

Apsland looked at Daniel and pointed to Olivia. "Please take care of your daughter."

Gomez released Patricia. "Ma'am, just give me a few seconds, please stay here."

Gomez and Apsland entered the dark garage. Apsland switched on the light, which flickered sporadically until it came on. Gomez knelt down next to the body.

"You're right," said Gomez to Apsland. "I shouldn't make promises I can't keep."

Harriet's fingernails were broken. Gomez had seen that before on victims, and he had also seen it on victims of the Life Swapper. But with the Life Swapper, no traces of DNA were ever found, or any blood besides that of the victim. These were defensive injuries. The other injuries were too extreme to even allocate a type.

Patricia gathered enough strength to put together a sentence. "It is George? Is it our son?"

Olivia hugged both Patricia and Daniel as they waited in agonized anticipation.

Gomez holstered his pistol. "No, ma'am, this is Harriet McKenzie. Can you please take your daughter away from here?" Patricia didn't respond. Apsland turned off the garage light and closed the door, and Gomez nodded at him approvingly. Gomez whispered to Apsland, "Jesus, thank God they didn't see this."

"OK," Gomez ushered them with his hands. "Let's all go upstairs."

"Our son is missing," groaned Patricia.

"Yes, George, we heard you calling for him," Gomez ushered again.

They all finally walked up the stairs into the dining room. Gomez talked along the way. "When did you notice him gone?" he looked at his watch. "It's just past eight-thirty now."

They all sat at the long dining table, Olivia on Patricia's lap.

Patricia turned to Daniel. "We went to bed with them at around seven forty-five."

Daniel nodded. "And I woke up, well, just a few minutes ago."

"When we heard the screaming?" asked Apsland.

"Yes," said Daniel. "I called out for George as soon as I woke up and noticed he wasn't in the bed."

"Sir, we've been outside your house since seven twenty-five tonight, and no one has either gone in or out of it," said Gomez.

"So he must still be inside?" said Patricia hopefully.

"Ma'am, would it be possible to have the little one watch some television?" asked Gomez.

Patricia nodded. "Honey," she said to Olivia, and they walked over to the television. "Dora the explorer" asked Olivia. Dora it was.

Patricia walked back to the table and sat down. Gomez was holding a photograph of the painting.

"You own this painting, right?" asked Gomez.

"Yes!" Patricia said. "Well no, not anymore." Daniel clenched his jaw, flexing the muscles.

"Ma'am?" asked Gomez.

"My husband threw it out, I asked him to." She looked at the picture and then at Daniel. She began to cry. "I knew it was that thing." She took the photograph from Gomez and slapped it on the table. "But we got rid of it, I don't understand." She shook her head and cried onto her arms as she spread her torso on the table. She looked at Daniel. "I don't understand, we got rid of it."

Daniel continued to clench his jaw. Patricia said again. "We got rid of it, but I should have known it wasn't over, not after what happened to you." She looked at Daniel. He didn't respond.

Patricia's eyes opened wide. She jumped up from the table, knocking over her chair. "You didn't get rid of it!"

Daniel remained seated. Patricia shouted again. Daniel just searched for words, he could choose any, but all of them were too pathetic and incriminating.

Instead, he displayed a remorseful face. Then he tried to lean forward and grab her wrists, and Patricia slapped his hands away. "Where is it?" she screamed.

Olivia was trying hard to ignore the conversation. She turned the television volume up and up.

A singing animated map appeared on the screen, walking around a spinning globe, singing, "I'm the map, I'm the map, I'm the map, I'm the map, I'm the maaaaaaap." This song was like a sick, twisted D.J. mix.

"I'm the map."

"I don't fucking believe you, Daniel."

"I'm the map."

"Where is that fucking thing?"

"I'm the map."

"I hate you, I hate you!"

"I'm the maaaaaaap."

Gomez jumped in. "Please, if we're to get your son back, let's try to focus." Gomez rushed over to Olivia. "Excuse me, young lady, you don't mind if I turn the volume down a little, do you?"

Olivia shook her head as she wiped her tears. "Tell Mommy she said something bad."

Patricia responded, "I know, honey, I said the F word, I'm sorry."

"No." Olivia turned to Patricia. "You said 'hate,' you said you hate Daddy."

Patricia ran over to Olivia and cuddled her. "Honey, I was just crazy because we need to find George, I wasn't thinking, I don't hate Daddy." Patricia looked over at Daniel with the hatred she told Olivia she didn't have. Olivia was consoled, but only to a degree. Resolution would have to wait.

"Sir, what did you do with the painting?" asked Gomez.

"I put in in the trunk of my car."

"So that's why you're parked outside." Patricia slumped into a chair and folded her arms. "Well, it didn't work, did it?"

Daniel shook his head and looked at Gomez. "What are you doing here? And why the interest in the painting?"

"Why?" snapped Patricia. "Because that painting—"

Gomez interrupted Patricia, holding out his hand. "Ma'am, please! Please let me respond."

Gomez remained silent a moment, just to make sure he would be listened to.

"Mr. Apsland and I are working on a case. It has remained open since 1972. It has only recently been discovered that whoever has owned this painting goes missing."

"Who is that person downstairs? You said Harriet, who is, was, she?" asked Patricia.

Gomez responded, taking care not to be overheard by Olivia. "She owned the painting, and the person who owned the painting before her was found dead at Harriet's address. It goes back to 1972 like this; that's the year it was painted. And now we traced the ownership to you, which was why we were outside tonight, and now your boy is missing."

"Except you don't just mean 'missing', do you? You mean missing and dead." Patricia stood up. "Are you telling me our son is going to be found dead like her? In some other house?"

Patricia opened a whole new fountain of tears from some sort of reserve tank that she had never had to use, until now. Warm tears, almost hot. She got up from her chair and walked around looking for sanctuary; finally, she lay on the cold floor, looking up at the ceiling.

Daniel knelt down beside her and cleared her hair from her face. He too began to cry.

"I'm so sorry," he said. "I'm so sorry."

He turned and looked up at Gomez. "What do we do? What *can* we do?"

Gomez took a deep breath. "Normally at this point, with a dead body, obviously a homicide, and a child missing, I would call the local police, and I will, but not just yet."

"Why not?" asked Patricia.

"Ma'am, as I said, no one left this house or entered it, we were outside."

"So what are you saying?" asked Patricia. "Are you saying that *it is* supernatural?"

Gomez avoided an immediate response. Instead he looked at Apsland and said, "One hand clapping, huh?"

Apsland looked at Patricia. "What do you think?"

"We bought it because it was supposed to be haunted, for fun, for a conversation piece." She wiped her face. "But it *is* haunted, damn it! *It is*, we have been through so much here since that thing arrived. I wanted to throw it away immediately but Daniel always defended it."

"Ah yes, the protector," said Apsland.

"Protector?" asked Daniel, but the moment he did so, he regretted it. "It's OK, it's OK, I get it, I get it."

Apsland denied Daniel his cancellation of the question and continued regardless. "Yes, a protector. A demonic entity will need a protector, otherwise their strategy will fail." Apsland looked in the direction of the garage. "Harriet, she was a protector."

"Then why did it kill her? I can't believe I'm saying this," said Daniel.

"Believe it, Daniel!" snarled Patricia.

"Who knows?" said Apsland. "Maybe she changed her mind. Did you? Did you change your mind, Dr. Leyden?"

Patricia looked at Daniel. "Nothing happened to you, nothing at all, until you said you'd get rid of it."

She looked at Apsland. "Yes, he changed his mind." Then she looked at Daniel. "But he changed it back again, and kept the damn thing in the car."

Daniel clasped his head tightly as he rested his elbows on his knees. He looked up, trying to ignore the stinging shame. "What do we do now?"

"Mrs. Leyden, to answer your question, I don't know if it is supernatural or not. What I do know is that conventional methods will continue to be employed. I'll see to that in a few moments, but after these last few days, and tonight, after what I've seen and heard, I'm gonna go with the unconventional first," said Gomez holding up his index finger.

He took some time to prepare his words. No one interrupted him, apart from Dora the Explorer who was very busy heroically assisting the family in keeping Olivia in a world as far away as possible from the real one.

"It has to be first," continued Gomez. "As soon as the local police and CSI arrive, they'll confiscate the painting and that might spell disaster. We might need it. In fact, I'm pretty sure of it. That's why I didn't call them as soon as I saw the body."

Gomez held up the photograph. "The artist, William Stoneham, has been incarcerated in the Binghamton Asylum for the criminally insane since the year he painted the painting. He's there for murdering his assistant, he pleads his innocence. We will go there tonight with the painting."

"Asylum? You mean, he's crazy?" asked Daniel. "Then how on earth can *he* help us?"

"On the contrary," said Apsland. "His being crazy, as you put it, leads one to assume he was driven crazy, and if it were this painting that did so, the painting he painted, then he must know something of the beast, and possibly a way to its belly." Gomez pointed at Daniel. "Get dressed." Daniel was not quick enough for Gomez, he pointed again. "Quickly!" Daniel turned and went sharply up the stairs.

Gomez pressed three digits on his cell phone. He walked over to Patricia and put his hand on her shoulder. "Please don't give up, please." He turned when he heard a voice on the line and quickly made his way into the hallway.

"Hello, I would like to report a homicide and missing person."

*

Gomez, Apsland and Daniel looked down at the painting in the trunk of the car.

"OK," said Gomez. He turned to Patricia, who was holding Olivia. "They have my details, and remember, all you know is we've gone to look for George, don't mention Stoneham, the painting, or anything else."

Patricia nodded. Gomez got in the car, Apsland was already inside.

Daniel leaned into the open window and asked Gomez, "Do I have time to speak to my wife?"

Gomez looked down the street. "Until we hear sirens and lights we're not going to leave your family alone anyway, so go ahead."

Daniel made his way to Patricia. Whatever spell had been cast over Daniel was gone. Patricia was thankful that her husband was back, or rather, she would have been thankful, but at this moment, it meant very little, and it was of no consolation whatsoever. Daniel knew that, and deserved it, he didn't parade his existence, as he knew his mere existence at this moment was an offense to her. He tried to remain as small and humble as he could. It was easy to feel this way, as he could feel no other way. He kissed Olivia on the back of her head.   Olivia turned. "Daddy, are you going to get George back now?"

Daniel looked at her, her words were for Daniel Leyden, the family man, nice guy, dependable. They were for her daddy, and she didn't want anyone else but this Daniel to respond, and he did. "Yes, honey, I am going to go and get George back."

Patricia drew in a cry but held it, she held on tight, though her eyes welled up.

Daniel ran his hands over Patricia's as he looked into her eyes.

Gomez called over to Daniel. "Can you hear that?" They both listened, distant sirens. "It's them," concluded Gomez. "Let's go."

Daniel released his hands from Patricia's and got in the back of the car. Gomez reversed out into the middle of the road, sitting across both lanes. "Put down your window," he said to Apsland. Apsland pressed the plastic chrome button. They both sat, weighing up the sirens from left to right. They got nearer and nearer. "The right?" asked Gomez.

"Yes," confirmed Apsland.

Gomez positioned the car facing the left.

"OK, let's go, they're here," said Apsland.

"Hold on, hold on, I'm not leaving them alone for a second." Gomez leaned over Apsland and called over to Patricia. "Mrs. Leyden, can you come down here to the curb, away from the house?"

Patricia nodded. She put Olivia down and they walked down to the curb.

Gomez switched off his lights and drove to the end of the road and parked behind some large trash cans, which largely obscured his car. The small residential area began to fill with blue flashing lights. Three blue-and-white squad cars pulled up outside of the Leydens' house.

Gomez, Apsland and Daniel twisted around in the car and looked out the back window through the gap the trash cans allowed. One of the officers, the only one not in uniform, greeted Patricia.

"OK, let's go," said Gomez, he quietly began to drive away, keeping his lights off. Daniel remained looking at Patricia and Olivia through the rear window, he watched them until a bend in the road took them out of his vision. Gomez flicked his eyes in the mirror. The same bend in the road allowed him to switch on his lights.

Mateusz. The Road to Binghamton.

That crash was fresh, thought Mateusz. Urska couldn't be far. He
was right, she wasn't; she was straight ahead, standing in the road
with her thumb out.

Mateusz roared, "Urska, Urska!" He was so happy, he
literally bounced in his seat like a child, he could die now, it didn't
matter, they were together.

But it did matter, it mattered to Urska. She ran into the woods
the moment she recognized the van.

"Urskaaaaaaaaaaaaaaa!" Mateusz screamed out of the
window, lengthening her short name.

He switched on his spot lamp and twisted it into the forest.
Urska appeared and disappeared between the trees and the trees
appeared and disappeared behind the spot lamp. Mateusz controlled
the speed, Urska knew she couldn't outrun the van. She stopped, so
did Mateusz.

"Don't get out!" she shouted. "Don't get out!"

"Why not?"

"If you get out, I will run into the forest and you will never find me." She paused and repeated: "Never!" She screamed it with such force that her whole body was engaged, not just her vocal cords; her torso, arms, legs were all forcibly recruited to ensure delivery of this message.

And it was delivered, but what Mateusz heard with his head was instantly overruled by his heart.

There was a momentary standoff, only momentary, as Urska read his next move. They both bolted at the same time, Urska into the forest and Mateusz out of his van. He fixed on her like a cheetah, nothing would break his fix on her. He knew if he did, it would mean he would lose her. He paced after her with more speed, with more agility, than he had ever had in his life. She didn't stand a chance.

He gained and gained. She turned, whimpering, devastated. Finally, she stopped. It was no use, she turned to him, panting. He stopped just a few trees away, but he stopped only for a second. Her face was so thin, though the beauty stripped from her had not affected her eyes, they were still as beautiful as they had always been. In two bounds he was with her, and he closed his arms around her thin body. She did not embrace him, her arms hung down by her sides limply.

She cried. "Why?"

He had an answer to her question, but he knew it would not be the right answer. There was no right answer.

"Because I love you," he said.

She placed her cold thin hands on his chest and pushed him back. Her force was only enough for him to understand that she was trying to push him away, not enough to actually do so. Nevertheless, he allowed her the space she desired.

She looked at him. "Then you're selfish." She stood back one pace. "Selfish!" She screamed. "You love me, you say you do."

"I do," said Mateusz genuinely.

"Then if you do, you should allow me to love you."

"I don't understand."

"My love for you is so strong, so full, that I cannot have you near me, you know what will happen. 'Whoever is with you will die too,' remember?" she said.

Mateusz nodded. "But…" he burst into tears and fell to his knees on some damp leaves. "I cannot leave you, I don't want to…"

Mateusz started to say, but snatched back the words of his genuine response just in time as he realized they would not serve him well. Instead he responded quite differently, now that his brain was trying to take care of his heart. "What she said was probably bullshit."

"Oh no," Urska spun around 360 degrees and slapped her hands down against her thighs. "What bullshit? What bullshit?" she shouted. "She was right, that witch was completely right, I am going to die."

"No, no, don't say that," cried Mateusz. "She wasn't right."

"Mateusz, those demons exist," said Urska. "I have seen them with my own eyes, I have felt them on my own skin. They live, they live," she exclaimed. "They have cursed me deep inside: I threw up eyeballs, Mateusz. Eyeballs!" she screamed. "Different colors, they were from the damned, and I heard those same damned people through the screams of that demon boy, trapped somewhere, they screamed through him, when he screams he sheds tears of blood." Urska knelt down beside Mateusz and began to kiss his tears as they ran down his face.

"But Urska," said Mateusz. "I cannot leave you, I don't care if I die."

"No, please, you have all of your life ahead, maybe I do too," she said, making her facial muscles smile. "I need to get to Stoneham and see what can be done."

"I will drive you," said Mateusz.

"No," pleaded Urska. "You can't, just leave me, it is not far now, I can walk, just go, please?"

Urska stood up and walked back toward the road. Mateusz ran his hands into the rotten leaves and squeezed them as tightly as he squeezed his eyes. He stood up and ran after Urska.

She was walking just off the tarmac under the first row of trees. He followed her. She could hear him behind her. "Go away!" she shouted up into the air.

Mateusz simply could not do that. Now his heart had taken over the situation, disregarding any consequences.

Urska turned in the street. "Go away." She stopped.

Mateusz walked to her like a scolded child. "I can't."

In the distance behind Mateusz's parked van were the high-suspended white lights of a truck, the small yellow lights dotted over the cab.

"Mateusz, here comes some transport, please, you must let me go."

"We will go together." He ignored her. "We will go together."

Urska looked into Mateusz's sad eyes.

The truck thundered down the narrow road, trimming the trees with the corners of its trailer. Mateusz saw an expression in Urska's eyes as she looked at him that he didn't expect to see. It was terror.

"No, no, please," she whispered to herself. She touched his tears with her right index finger and then turned her hand and looked at it. "No, no, you can't!" she screamed, she hid her finger in her fist. The truck thundered upon them.

Urska gently touched Mateusz' cheek and whispered, "I love you."

She took three steps out from the trees into the road and into the enormous chrome grill of the truck.

Mateusz was still, his eyes fixed on where she had been. Without moving his eyes from the spot, he walked into the road. He knew what had happened. Instead, he calmly called out Urska's name as if searching for her. He walked out onto the empty road, he turned to the left and watched the tail lights of the truck disappear.

"Urska?" He walked around calling for her. He said her name over and over again. He ran down the empty road and back up again. He turned and looked back down the road. To his left, lying in some leaves, was Urska. Mateusz walked toward her. He couldn't hear anything, not even his own voice, he was shouting her name, he knew he was shouting as he could see the spray coming from his mouth as he screamed, his breath spiralling slowly in the cold air. He knelt down and cradled her in his arms. He looked up through the trees screaming, and then looked back down at Urska, her eyes open and still. Her face was no longer thin and stressed, she was again beautiful. She had no damage, no blood at all on her body, apart from on her right index finger. Mateusz looked at it. He instantly remembered she had touched his tears and then looked at her finger. *'No no, please.' 'I love you.' 'When he screams, he sheds tears of blood.' 'I love you.' 'I love you.' 'I love you.' 'I love you.'*

The words were too much to contain internally, he continued aloud. "I love you, I love you, I love you…" so primeval were his cries, they transcended species, in this vast forest both vegetation

and animal were hit by his wall of pain as it echoed through the
infinite trees.

The Road to Binghamton

On the left was a large industrial steel complex. Thousands of brand-new fork-lift trucks were lined up like little yellow and red soldier ants awaiting inspection.

Gomez's car sped past. The complex disappeared from view in a blur, eyes flicking, too fast to even understand the name of the company, a few seconds later the street lights also disappeared. Now they were confronted with mile after mile of forest.

Gomez put on his full beam.

The trees reminded Apsland of his visit to Pompeii, the casts from those ash figures frozen in their moment of death. Those twisted trees looking down at them seemed resentful at being so rudely exposed in this offensive light, pointing scornfully their condemning fingers.

The sense of impending doom in the car was obvious, and no analysis was necessary. They each felt like D-Day marines, they knew they would face unknown forces. But it was *they* who were bringing on the fight, *they* were the aggressor. Then why did they feel that they were being pulled along?

Gomez felt he could almost switch off the engine and they'd get there just the same.

No, whatever was in store for them at Binghamton would not be laid out in any plan. So Gomez kept it simple, just speak to Stoneham, speak to Stoneham.

If you have a dead body in your trunk, it's doubtful you'd have much inclination for conversation on a long road trip. What they had in the trunk was and felt infinitely worse. Daniel did not speak, he just wished each mile to be gone, each second he wanted passed in order to get to the asylum. He was trying to avoid speculating over the plight of his son. It didn't work, he thought of his son constantly, but through sheer will power he imagined resolving the situation, with a good outcome. Only by employing this strategy could he endure the frustrating miles, and the silence. He forced his mind to wander to escape his torture. He stared out at the copy-and-paste landscape in front of them, a mapping of the same hypnotic trees over and over again like a looping screensaver. He was day-dreaming, he was dreaming that he was walking a dog, a dog he knew well but had never seen before, it was on a leash behind him.

Gomez jumped. "Yes?"

Apsland had asked him a question, the question was: "What do you really think?" Gomez had heard it but he was trembling, he had been asleep, albeit with his eyes open, but he knew he hadn't been in any conscious state for some time, it was a miracle they were not all wrapping a tree with tin foil. Gomez peeked into the rear view mirror to see if Daniel had noticed, but he was lost in deep thought.

"About what?" asked Gomez.

"You still believe the culprit is physical, don't you?"

"Only something physical can do what was done to Mrs. McKenzie," answered Gomez in a low whisper.

Apsland didn't respond. Gomez continued. "You believe this murderer, the Life Swapper, is something, as you put it, 'of another realm,' yes?"

"Yes I do," said Apsland.

"Then let me ask you this, of all your years in your field what have you seen? I mean, really seen?"

Apsland hesitated. "It's not always about seeing, it is about feeling."

"Ah, no," mocked Gomez. "That's a bail out. It's *all* about seeing, if you haven't seen anything in all those years, then maybe there's nothing to see." He shook his head. "Ha, feeling!"

"You ridicule feeling," Apsland paused, debating if he should continue. He chose to do so. "Then why is your stomach churning? Why are you deathly frightened to go on? Where has your mind been for these last fifty-seven miles? You've been little more than a passenger, only some automatic process controlling the wheel."

So Apsland *had* noticed that Gomez was absent. Gomez shrugged, his wits were still not fully functioning after his zone out, so he figured a shrug would be his best bet.

Apsland insisted. "And why is every part of your body telling you not to continue?" Apsland looked at Gomez. "And don't tell me it's because of Harriet McKenzie back there, you're a homicide detective, you barely blinked when you saw her. No, something is scaring you like no other investigation you've ever undertaken. You look ahead at the road but you too can feel the wretched thing in the trunk, you feel it! Don't you? And it scares you!"

"It is very difficult to believe all this," said Daniel.

Apsland turned quickly and scornfully, he furrowed his brow and pointed at him. "And you," said Apsland as he leaned forward. "That dog, that dog wants … to … eat ... you."

Daniel was rendered incapacitated by this, so shocked he managed only to cough and sit up in his seat.

They continued on in silence. Eventually, Gomez's lights picked up a sign pointing to Binghamton. They turned into a narrow lane, its asphalt pot-holed, almost more hole than asphalt. On the right the trees suddenly stopped, there to the right on an incline was Binghamton.

They clambered out of their vehicle, verifying what they could see through the windows. Binghamton was abandoned.

It stood arching over them like a frozen black tidal wave.

"Jesus!" shouted Daniel.

"I don't understand," said Gomez.

The weeds stood shoulder height. The roof had huge chunks missing, like it had suffered a brutal D.I.Y lobotomy, hardly any windows were intact, those that were, were opaque like cataracts.

Daniel picked up a stone and flung it at one of the last cataracts. He missed, he walked backwards and sat on the hood of Gomez's car. He put his head in his hands and spouted random words.

"And now? My son? This Stoneham? What? Where now?"

From the narrow lane, the sound of an engine could be heard, quickly followed by headlights. Gomez walked into the path of the vehicle and pointed to his left behind his vehicle. He did this with the authority only law enforcement have mastered.

The vehicle obliged and rolled up behind Gomez's car.

"My God," said Daniel. "What the hell are you doing here?"

Mateusz got out of the van.

"Who is this man?" asked Gomez.

"I am Mateusz."

Daniel grabbed Mateusz's shoulders and then instantly let go, he turned to Gomez and Apsland. "This man is a ghost hunter, my wife employed him and his girlfriend."

Mateusz hung his head.

Daniel continued. "My God, Mateusz." Daniel started to whimper. "If I had only listened." He again grabbed Mateusz's shoulders. "If I had just listened, my son is gone, if I had just listened, it wouldn't have happened."

Mateusz continued to look at the ground.

Daniel continued. "Did you find Urska?"

Mateusz looked up. "Yes, yes I found her."

"OK, OK, that's good," said Daniel.

Gomez and Apsland were reading Mateusz much more successfully than Daniel was.

"Yes, yes good," continued Mateusz pointing to the van. "Go and say hello, she's in the back of the van."

Daniel nodded. He walked over to the van, followed closely by Gomez and Apsland.

"Allow me," said Gomez. Gomez opened the door, there, on a gray army surplus blanket, was her corpse.

"Say hello then!" screamed Mateusz. He walked toward Daniel. Gomez quickly jumped in his path. "Why don't you say hello, go on, you foolish prick!"

Gomez didn't ask Mateusz to stop, he just held him physically back, he had the feeling that whatever this young man had to say should be said. "If you had just listened? Huh? If you had just listened? If you had just listened to your wife, then my Urska wouldn't have been cursed, she wouldn't be dead."

Mateusz broke into tears. Apsland took him from Gomez's grip. "Come with me."

Apsland walked Mateusz away from Daniel. "She killed herself?" asked Apsland.

Mateusz nodded. "How did you know?"

"Because she is not cursed." Apsland put his hand on Mateusz' shoulder. "She's free."

"I want to speak to Stoneham," said Mateusz, and then he turned to Daniel. "I will destroy the painting, and if you try to stop me…" he waved his finger. "I will kill you."

"What Stoneham? What Stoneham?" pled Daniel. "Look, the place is dead, it's abandoned."

"No it's not," said Mateusz. "It has two faces, the abandoned west wing and the working east wing, we must go to the other side."

The Visit

They stood under a huge archway. Daniel clutched the painting like a life buoy.

Above them, in forged rusted iron letters, was a sign that read: "New York State Inebriate Asylum. 1858."

Gomez pressed the weathered entry buzzer. After a few seconds, an electric buzz ran through the oak door. Gomez pushed.

They walked in tentatively. They stood in a large cavernous hallway. The architecture was gothic and unforgiving, marble goblins looked down at them from plinths high above, the 19th-century equivalent of security cameras.

Occasional distant screams and muffled crying could be heard echoing off the cold walls.

A thin, black female guard came toward them. Gomez held up his badge.

"Good evening, ma'am. We are here to see a Mr. Stoneham, a William Stoneham."

The lady stared blankly at Gomez. He couldn't work out if she had understood and thought he was joking or she didn't understand at all. He repeated his question.

Again she just stared.

"Ma'am, do you understand me?" asked Gomez. He looked quizzically at Apsland. "What's with this woman?"

He continued. "We're here to see William Stoneham. Do—you—understand?"

"No, she doesn't understand."

Gomez, Apsland and Mateusz turned sharply. Governor Lockwood, a large-framed black woman with striking silver hair, smiled at the group over her bifocals. She held out her large hand and began to shake each person's hand in turn.

She turned to the guard. "That's all, thanks sugar."

"Is she a guard?" asked Gomez.

"No, no, she's an inmate, we dress her up as a guard and she's as happy as a flea in a doghouse. You know it's after hours for visiting?"

"Yes, ma'am. I'm Detective Hector Gomez from Boston PD, homicide."

"Boston?"

"That's right," confirmed Gomez. "We have a case, a homicide case, and it is urgent that we speak to William Stoneham."

"Do you know it's 11:30pm?"

"I'm sorry," replied Gomez, with an apologetic smile and a raise of his shoulders.

"Stoneham huh?" Governor Lockwood chuckled insincerely. "I knew it would be him."

"Ma'am?" asked Gomez.

"I saw you all with a painting and I knew it was him."

"Well, we have a missing person and it is crucial that we ask Mr. Stoneham some questions, you might be saving someone's life."

"Don't you need some kind of warrant or permission first?" she insisted.

"Yes, ma'am, but only if the acting person were to deny access, only then would we have to apply for that, and by then our killer, or kidnapper, could be long gone. Time is critical, as I said, you could be helping to save someone's life," said Gomez.

Governor Lockwood pondered the predicament; her eyes flicking around, chasing imaginary flies. She fixed on one, she had it.

"OK, first come to my office, let's make this official."

"Agreed, that's fine, always a good idea to keep things aboveboard," said Gomez.

"Hm, if you say so," said Governor Lockwood. "I'm just covering my ass."

She turned and walked off. They all followed, Gomez walked alongside her, Mateusz and Apsland behind them next to each other and finally Daniel formed the tip of this inverted triangle. He clutched the painting and looked around anxiously like a child afraid someone would steal his candy.

Governor Lockwood's heels clacked sharply on the floor. They made their way through the corridors, passing inmates in differing conditions of sanity, watched by the very occasional guard. They came out to a cross roads and took a right. They began to walk down the longest corridor that any of them had ever seen. Governor Lockwood had given this tour before, and she knew what they were all thinking. "It's called 'the mirrors'," she remarked.

No one replied. "The mirrors," she repeated. "It's 660 feet, one eighth of a mile."

"That's two hundred meters," muttered Mateusz.

"That's right. Long enough that you can't see the end, they call it mirrors, you know, like when you put two mirrors face to face, it's just the same, I mean even mathematically it's the same, not just how it would appear, but factually the same … something about field of vision and distance, anyway, you get the idea."

"It's diabolical," said Apsland.

The tip of their triangle was slightly longer. Another had joined. An inmate shuffled along behind Daniel. Daniel looked back over his shoulder to see a dishevelled man in a white gown shuffling behind him looking at Daniel's heels. "Excuse me, Governor Lockwood?" asked Daniel.

Governor Lockwood turned and stopped. "Mr. Jasper? Sir."

The man just studied Daniel's heels as if they were filet mignon. Governor Lockwood walked over to a wall phone and pressed a button. "You're needed," she said. "I'm by B3, well, between B3 and 4." The moment she said that, the squeaking of rubber sneakers caught up to the group. Two burly guards arrived.

"Governor?" asked one of the men.

"Mr. Jasper here wants to go back to his room," she said.

The two men grabbed Mr. Jasper's arms, one each side, and lifted him. They walked him backwards down the corridor suspending him a few inches above the floor. "Nice doggy," he said.

Apsland started on hearing this.

"Nice doggy," the man repeated as he floated backwards down the hall. "Come here, doggy."

Apsland looked at Daniel and then down at his feet. Daniel looked down at his own feet too.

"We don't have much time," said Apsland.

Governor Lockwood turned and began to walk again, the group followed.

"What was that?" asked Daniel.

"What happened?" asked Mateusz.

"You're a ghost hunter, Mateusz. Tell Dr. Leyden about dogs, he has one following him," said Apsland.

Mateusz's eyes were in a constant state of tearing. Merely being spoken to made the tears trickle out down his face. His expression didn't display emotion, that was all bottled up, as it was for Daniel, there was work to do. Yet the rush of emotion forced its way through, the tears came out regardless of any attempt at emotional control.

"Demonic dogs, or hellhounds as you call them in America, are said to be employed by demons for four reasons: one, to guard an entrance to the world of the dead, which is why they are usually found in graveyards; two, sometimes they are assigned to hunt for lost souls; three, they are employed to guard supernatural treasures; and four, to guard supernatural creatures. In your hands, you hold all of those reasons."

Mateusz walked away from Daniel.

Daniel called in the direction of Apsland, "You said it wanted to eat me?"

Mateusz laughed. "I hope it does."

Daniel ran up and grabbed Mateusz's shoulder. Mateusz spun around and tried to punch him but clumsily missed. Daniel slipped on the hard floor, they both fell over, and the painting fell to the floor. Gomez and Apsland jumped in to break up the fight as Governor Lockwood blew her whistle. Daniel and Mateusz gripped each other's shirts as they rolled on the floor.

"You blame me," said Daniel. "You blame me, but I didn't believe."

"If it wasn't for you, my Urska would still be alive!" screamed Mateusz.

"No!" screamed Daniel "If it wasn't for *you*. *You* believe, that means *you* should have looked out for her, she was *your* girlfriend and *you* believed, *I* didn't so *I* had no reason to think something could happen, because *I* didn't believe, understand?"

"No, no, you're a protector, it's just that you were and still are too stupid to realize that is what you were."

Three guards arrived and helped to finally break them apart.

Mateusz dusted himself off. Daniel didn't bother, he just picked up the painting.

"And even if I was this 'protector' then it wasn't something I did intentionally. Go on, yes, say I was stupid, I don't care, at least my mistakes were done in innocence, but you knew, you believed." Daniel stopped speaking as he didn't want to cry. His eyes filled with tears and both his lips quivered uncontrollably. "My son is missing. Please, help me get him back."

Mateusz slumped against the wall. He closed his eyes, tears fell directly onto the floor. Mateusz nodded, and Daniel placed his hand on Mateusz's shoulder.

Governor Lockwood turned to Gomez. "Is it this man's child that's missing?"

"Yes, ma'am, yes it is," said Gomez.

The group recommenced their walk down the corridor. Governor Lockwood unbuckled a set of keys the size of a large orange. Inserting a thick Chubb key, she turned it what seemed a ludicrous amount of revolutions. Then she took out another key and finally gained entry.

Her office was dominated by an enormous black cast-iron radiator, which didn't work.

On the walls were etchings of the building and a blueprint showing the layout. She turned to a tambour filing cabinet.

Eventually, she teased out a paper titled "Visitor".

"Can I have your badge, Detective Gomez?"

Gomez handed her his badge. She sat down at her desk and began to fill out the form. There were three chairs, so enough for most of them to take a seat, but she didn't invite them to, and no one asked. She wanted their visit over.

She turned the paper around and handed Gomez a pen. Gomez signed his name. "You know why Stoneham is incarcerated here, right?" she asked, peering up at them all.

An unsteady ensemble of nodding heads said yes.

She stood up and pointed to the blueprint. "Well, the reason he's here is the reason he's there." She tapped a small area seemingly at the end of a long corridor.

"High security," she said. She looked at Daniel. "The man who saw an invisible dog?"

"Yes?" said Daniel.

"He killed his family. He owned a bakery; he baked them all alive. Locked them in a huge oven and came back in the morning."

"Why are you telling us this?" asked Gomez.

"Mr. Jasper, the baker, he's medium security, that's the only reason I'm telling you."

"I see," said Gomez. "That's why you had me sign the form."

"Well, it's a high-security area, it's just for insurance, but we don't want to be sued now, do we? Just in case one of them bites you." She smiled. "Or bashes your heads in with a fire extinguisher."

She picked up a phone and spoke into it while looking the group in the eye one by one. She put the phone down. "Your guards will be here in a few minutes, and we'll escort you down to Stoneham."

The Work of the Devil

The two guards and Governor Lockwood dictated the pace of their walk. The pace was "Get them out of here." This part of the building was below ground, it had low ceilings, the corridor felt more like that of a submarine. The walls were curved and painted duck-egg blue in glossy paint. In an alcove to the left, they passed an area that looked like an abandoned kitchen, open, with no door or walls. There was a small combined chair and writing desk, the kind you find at school. The detective in Gomez immediately noticed the scrapes on the chair's metal frame. Chain marks.

Whatever that desk had been used for, it wasn't for writing.

They arrived at the end of this claustrophobic tunnel at a gray metal door. At each side of the door stood two more guards, both with their arms folded. Governor Lockwood nodded toward the door.

"I don't intend to have you stay here for a second more than you need to. They get upset with new faces poking around."

"Thank you for your cooperation," said Gomez.

"These men will continue to guard the door. I don't know what you want to see him for and I don't want to know, just make it fast."

"Is he already inside?" asked Gomez.

Governor Lockwood nodded. She beckoned to a guard to open the door. The guard first looked through a small drop hatch before unbolting the door. The usual multiple revolutions of his key were necessary. The guard pushed the heavy door open but remained outside. The door opened to revealed William Stoneham, in a windowless, narrow room. One end of the room had no light bulb, rendering it so dark you couldn't see the back wall. Stoneham sat at the other end, facing the dark end. He sat at a blue-checked Formica table surrounded by white walls, in a white straitjacket, his white beard balancing the color scheme. His eyes were fixed on something perceptible only to him.

Gomez took the first few steps inside. He was followed by Apsland, Mateusz and Daniel. Governor Lockwood and the guards remained outside.

"He's shackled!" said Gomez.

"Yes, the straitjacket is for your own protection," replied Governor Lockwood soberly. She took a deep breath and continued. "These two guards will remain outside at this door." She closed the door.

There were only three chairs in total. Gomez, defying a cliché, picked one up, spun it around and sat in front of Stoneham, leaning his arms on the backrest.

Apsland took a seat. Mateusz leaned against the cold wall. Daniel placed the painting against the wall next to the door and then stood behind Gomez.

The sound of the keys turned in the door. *Jesus, they don't take any chances*, thought Gomez.

Gomez explained to Stoneham who he was, he showed Stoneham his badge and explained the situation factually. Apsland shook his head, feeling that this was the wrong approach.

"Detective Gomez?" said Apsland. "You don't need to approach this man as if he were a skeptic. You don't need to appease him by avoiding the unbelievable."

Gomez continued, "So we believe that a killer might be following your work and committing these crimes."

Stoneham ignored all of this. Apsland stood up sharply and spun around 360 degrees, displaying his impatience.

"I have to agree with Mr. Apsland," said Daniel.

Mateusz stared at Stoneham. "He's not even with us," said Mateusz. "Look at him." Mateusz walked up to him and waved his hand in front of Stoneham's face. "Nothing, look."

"Can I sit here?" Daniel asked Gomez. They switched places. Daniel looked into Stoneham's eyes and Stoneham avoided eye contact. This was a sign that he was indeed aware. "I know you can hear me," Daniel said. He took out his wallet and held a photo in front of Stoneham. "This is my son." Stoneham stared straight ahead, ignoring the photograph.

"He's just seven years old."

Stoneham did not respond. Daniel continued. "He has been taken, into your painting," then he groaned. "And it's my fault, my fault." Daniel thumped his fist on his knee. "I knew, well some part of me knew, that painting, your painting *was indeed* cursed, but instead I ignored my feelings and, and I wouldn't listen to anyone," he began to squeeze his emotions in a grimace. "I just doomed my son to death. Or worse than death maybe," he screamed. "It has killed, now I believe it, my housekeeper Manuela, and this man's girlfriend. At my house is the corpse of another victim. Only you can end this, only you."

Daniel looked back into Stoneham's eyes. Stoneham was now looking at the photograph of George. "It's not your fault," he whispered. "It's not your fault."

He turned to Apsland. "You know, don't you?"

Apsland nodded.

"But there's nothing *I* can do," said Stoneham.

Daniel wiped his face. "But sir, you are our last hope."

"No, no please don't ask anything of me, please."

"Don't ask?" said Daniel as he wrapped his hands around his wrapped forearms like handcuffs. "Then George is lost, gone."

"I can't help you," said Stoneham. "Please go."

"Go?" shouted Daniel. "Go where? Why won't you help?"

"Go!" shouted Stoneham. "You're all in danger." He began to rock back and forth in his small chair."

"*The Hands Resist Him*," screamed Daniel, "is your creation, your creation."

Stoneham rocked back and forth violently, he began to shake his head in an attempt to un-hear the words, but Daniel repeated them.

"Your creation!" he screamed over and over.

"My creation? My creation?" screamed Stoneham. "No, no, no, not mine, not mine."

"Yes, yours," shouted Daniel. "You painted it, you."

"Not mine, not mine!" screamed Stoneham.

In the turmoil, Apsland stood up and grabbed the painting from the wall. He walked over to Stoneham and put the painting inches from his face.

"There is your signature," said Apsland.

Stoneham flew back in the chair onto the floor, he tried to scurry backwards, kicking his heels on the hard shiny floor as he struggled to get purchase. "Get it away from me, away," he screamed.

The two guards entered the room, complaining about the commotion. They made their way toward Stoneham. Gomez stopped them. This standoff turned into a minor scuffle. It only stopped when Gomez shouted, "Stop! Get out of here, this is a police matter, it does not concern you, out! If we need you, I will call for you, understand? Now out!"

The guards acquiesced and left the room, but their down-turned mouths made their opinions known. "OK," said one. "But we ain't locking the door."

"Whatever," said Gomez.

Mateusz helped Stoneham back to his seat. Stoneham placed his forehead on the table, whimpering. "Keep that away from me."

Apsland placed it behind Stoneham against a wall.

Daniel kneeled down beside Stoneham. What little resolve he had was now gone, he free-fell without a parachute into a total breakdown. His body could no longer hold up his head, he fell on his side onto the cold floor, and tears ran down the sides of his face. He held up George's photograph and then clutched it against his chest. "I'm so sorry Son, I'm so sorry."

Daniel stared at the ceiling. Each of the group stared at something, a wall, a chair leg, a door, no one looked at Stoneham or each other.

"My first commission, my first commission," whispered Stoneham. All eyes flinched slightly more open. No one said a thing; they didn't want to break the spell.

"My first commission." Stoneham's body quivered, he bowed his head down low like a dog about to be chastised by a cruel master.

"I cannot remember painting anything. I had been working on it for what seemed an eternity, but an eternity with no sense of time about it. I didn't know what I had painted. I had to look at it. I suddenly felt devastated, as if I had lost part of myself forever. I felt cheated, I felt I had committed the most evil of crimes. I collapsed, dropping my brush. From that moment, my life changed. I was consumed by the painting."

He paused and turned around looking for the painting. He saw it from the corner of his eye against the wall. He turned back.

"Then it began. Each night I would be visited by the doll and the boy, they tormented me, they wanted me to follow them to..." he smiled ironically. "Finish my work."

He leaned forward, squeezing his eyes tight shut and then opening them in revelation. "I refused! Abigail, my assistant, was standing behind me, screaming that I should burn it. With all my being, with all of the soul I had left, the soul that was still mine, I roared out to that cursed painting. I said, 'I will never do the Devil's work again!'"

He exhaled in all-consuming anguish and squirmed in his chair, physically recoiling at a diabolical memory. "Then I watched Abigail in the mirror standing behind me. Her head began to twist, and twist and twist and twist and twist..."

Stoneham became hysterical. He shouted the word over and over. Daniel grabbed Stoneham, breaking him from his hysteria. "Please, sir! Help my son."

Apsland calmly interjected, "Sir, you must end this."

Stoneham looked at them. "Do you realize what you're asking of me?"

"Yes," said Gomez. "Yes, sir we do, death."

"Death?" said Stoneham. "Is that what you think? What you're asking from me is far worse than death."

"I have no right to ask," said Daniel. "I, I put him at risk."

"No," said Stoneham. "If the painting had never existed you would have done no such thing, I made it exist." He turned to Apsland and looked at him. "How do you intend to proceed?"

"A séance. I must begin a communication with them," said Apsland.

"There's a much quicker way," said Stoneham. "A sure way, do you have a match?"

"Yes. Yes, I do."

"Then light a match and burn the painting."

"No, no you can't," said Daniel. "Then George will be lost forever."

"They will never allow the painting to be destroyed, they will come to prevent it, and we need them to come," said Stoneham.

"Are you sure?"

"The painting cannot be destroyed," said Stoneham.

Apsland walked over to the painting and kneeled down. He took out a matchbook, and struck a match. He cupped it with his hands and lowered it to the bottom right-hand corner. A sharp gust of wind blew out the flame.

Apsland struck again. He held the flame at the corner of the canvas.

Gomez squinted. In the dark corner at the end of the long room, two shapes gradually became visible, like the developing of an old negative in a darkroom. Any doubts Gomez had were now gone. The two dark spectres gradually came nearer, not through any physical movement on their part, yet they were nearer.

The boy opened his mouth. A sudden rush of stagnant air blew through the room, blowing out Apsland's match. This foul air carried the sound of agony with it. Mateusz was fixed to the spot, he internalized his terror and began to make small roars deep within his chest. He could see before him just what had cursed his Urska, he could hear the sound of those lost souls as they screamed from the boy.

Stoneham turned and shouted to make himself heard through the violence of this visitation. "Close your eyes, close your eyes!"

They all closed their eyes, the foul wind battering their bodies. The guards, on hearing the commotion, tried to enter the room, but an invisible force held the door shut.

Stoneham's moment had arrived. He stood upon his trembling legs and walked toward the boy and the doll. The group kept their eyes tightly shut. Mateusz held his hands over his ears to avoid hearing the desperate pleas of the doomed souls.

The demonic boy opened his arms for Stoneham. Stoneham looked into the black vacant eyes.

The intensity of the crying reached a climax. Upon the violent wind the room was suddenly filled with a blast even stronger, sending Mateusz over onto the floor. The lights flickered with such an intensity that some exploded, then everything went quiet. The guards fell into the room and scrambled to their feet, they looked around the room, but Stoneham was missing.

Each of them was silent in disbelief. A few moments past like the aftermath f a hurricane, then they heard sobbing coming from the darkened corner of the room.

Sitting in the corner was a small boy, his hands and head on his knees.

"George?" exclaimed Daniel. He ran to his son and pulled him up into his arms into his chest. George's muffled screams penetrated deep into Daniel's chest, screaming directly to Daniel's heart.

"It's OK son, it's OK." Daniel caressed his son's hair as he held him tightly.

Governor Lockwood stood at the door with her arms folded. "What the hell is going on here?"

Gomez stood up. He had nothing. He raised his hands and shook his head, hoping something would spring to mind. He was too slow, and she continued.

"Where's Stoneham? And who's the boy? What the? the Son? Where the hell did he come from?"

She looked at Apsland, then Mateusz, then Daniel. As no explanation came from them, she looked at the guards. "What happened?"

"A whole lotta screaming, the lights went out and we couldn't get in, we—" said a guard.

Governor Lockwood didn't let him finish. "I'm calling the police."

"There's no need for that. I am officially on this case. I will handle the situation here," said Gomez in the vain hope she might buy it.

She made it clear that didn't work. "Detective Gomez, I don't care if you're the D.A., one of my patients is missing and went missing in a guarded room with one door and no windows, and now in his place there's a young boy, obviously that man's son," she said, waving a hand at Daniel. She paused, looking at their expressions. Something had happened; she could see that. "In all honesty, I don't know whether to call the police or a witch doctor."

She slammed the door, her heels tapped out of audio range as she marched off to call the police. George broke from his father's embrace. His entire face was wet with tears.

"Daddy?" He looked at Daniel in a way he had never looked at him before. "Daddy, there were dead people, hundreds, but they weren't dead like Granny was, they were…"

He began to cry again. He pulled at Daniel's shirt. He screamed, "…alive!" he howled back into Daniel's chest.

Daniel was powerless to explain. He could only offer his love, his affection. He had no words to explain, as there were no words.

George pushed back from the embrace again. "Daddy, who was that man? Someone, a man, he came and saved me. He knew my name, he told me to run to the light. He had no fingers."

"No fingers?" urged Apsland.

George shook his head.

The guard looked at Apsland. "Mister, the man the boy's talking about is Stoneham. He cut off all his fingers years ago."

Apsland closed his eyes, recalling Stoneham's words. "I shall never do the Devil's work again."

Good Riddance

The rusted arched entrance to the asylum was full of the flashing of the blue lights of three squad cars, all parked in unnecessarily dramatic angles to each other.

The police officers were taking statements. The most enthusiastic of the witnesses were the two guards. They were busy re-enacting the whole thing to the amusement of an officer, who bit his pen to stop himself smiling.

Daniel sat on one of the entrance steps. George was on his lap, wrapped in a gray blanket. Daniel said, "I love you," into his cell phone, and smiled. He was immune to the turmoil around him. His son was back, Daniel was back, he felt centered again. The events had knocked him off of his axis, now, with his son in his arms, his wife's relief, and his relief of this burden, he could finally relax.

The first thing Gomez thought on seeing Detective Vaden was, *you've been watching too many movies*. Vaden had blond hair gelled back, a black jacket and a toothpick sticking out of the corner of his mouth.

"So, Detective Gomez," said Detective Vaden, looking at Gomez's identification. "This lady," he indicated Governor Lockwood, who stood on a step behind Gomez, making her tower above him. Her arms were folded and she tapped her right foot, burning holes into the back of Gomez's head. Vaden continued in a whisper. "She wants someone arrested, and I've gotta say, after the statements we've heard, well, it's a real problem."

Gomez responded as flatly as he could. "I'll take responsibility."

Detective Vaden took his toothpick out of his mouth and held it like a tiny conductor's baton. "Are you saying that you stand by these statements? Including your own account of Stoneham disappearing? And this boy showing up?"

Gomez paused. He knew he'd have to commit one way or another, but he didn't want to ruin his career. So he did what any honest person would do. He lied. "Yes, I do. I'm not sure how it happened, maybe Stoneham got out, because the guards had unlocked the door. Maybe the boy ran in. We had our eyes closed."

Detective Vaden didn't say a word. He didn't need to, his little toothpick did all the talking. He placed it back in his mouth quickly and precisely. He was good at using it for communication. Gomez clearly heard, 'Bullshit' as he did so.

Detective Vaden looked at his notes and shrugged. "Well, what do I care? It'll be you standing up in court with this, not me."

He took his toothpick out again and made small jabs like a dart player before a throw. "You know I'm gonna have to take them all in." He looked over at Daniel and George. "Even those two."

"That boy needs to be reunited with his mother and sister," said Gomez.

"I don't even know if that's the father," responded Detective Vaden.

"It's your call," said Gomez.

"That's right! It's my call," said Detective Vaden. He punctuated this by snapping his toothpick and flicking it on the ground.

Gomez turned and saw Apsland and Mateusz standing together in a hushed conference. He walked over to them as casually as he could.

"Where is it?" asked Apsland.

"I told Leyden to drop it," said Gomez.

"Why?" asked Mateusz.

Gomez leaned in. "Because they will seize it for evidence."

"Where did he drop it?" asked Apsland.

"You remember that kind of kitchen area just before we arrived at Stoneham's cell?" said Gomez. They both nodded.

"What do you want to do with it?" asked Apsland.

"Destroy it," said Gomez.

"Destroy evidence?" said Apsland. "I take it that means you no longer believe there is a rational explanation?"

Gomez didn't respond.

"I will destroy it," said Apsland. Before Gomez had a chance to respond, Mateusz turned and ran back inside the asylum. Gomez chased after him, calling to Apsland, "Stay there."

Detective Vaden shouted to Gomez. "What's going on over there?"

"I've got it," responded Gomez, hovering at the entrance.

"By the way, so you know, I've put an APB out on Stoneham," said Detective Vaden.

Gomez nodded in approval and gave a thumbs-up before disappearing back inside.

He ran back through the main hall and down the small set of stairs to the basement. He immediately ceased running. Mateusz was being held by a guard.

"It's OK," said Gomez, catching his breath. "He's with me."

"Oh?" said the unimpressed guard. "And who's with you?"

Gomez smiled as he rested his hands on his knees.

"You're out of shape, mister," continued the guard.

Gomez pulled out his badge. The guard released Mateusz. Gomez thanked him with a nod and smile as he walked past, grabbing Mateusz and marching him down the corridor.

"What the hell are you doing?" asked Gomez *sotto voce*, in a discreet but firm growl.

"*I* will destroy that bastard thing," said Mateusz defiantly. "It destroyed my Urska, now *I* will destroy *it*."

"If it *can* be destroyed," said Gomez.

"Never mind what Stoneham said, I will find a way," said Mateusz resolutely.

Leaning against the abandoned school desk was the painting. Mateusz picked it up.

"Just avoid the main entrance." Said Gomez as he looked around. "Just find a way out before you attempt to destroy it, there are too many guards here."

Mateusz looked at the painting and nodded.

"I have to get back out there," said Gomez. "Once I'm out there without you, they'll come in here to look for you." Gomez looked back down the corridor. "Hopefully they haven't already taken that step. You'd better get going."

Mateusz ran off, the painting under his arm. Gomez slowly began to walk back down the corridor.

Mateusz chose a different set of steps to get back to ground level. He came up in a kitchen area behind some stainless steel carts, lit by the neon-blue light of a fly zapper.

He quietly pushed the carts away, allowing him to move through the large kitchen. He opened the kitchen door. It let out onto yet another corridor. To the right, it was clear and lit by rectangular ceiling lights. The left was cluttered with more kitchen appliances covered in dust, layers of it, the same rectangular ceiling lights ran along the ceiling, but they had long since been switched off.

He went left, away from any signs of life. As he made his way along the corridor, he passed abandoned rooms on either side. The air grew colder as the broken windows gave refuge to the outside elements.

He knew where he was. He passed one room and noticed the opaque glass. He was looking from within the building's other face, the derelict face.

He went into the room and climbed out through one of the glassless windows onto the back of a rotten dried wooden bench.

He was out. He ran down the embankment to his van. He jumped in and placed the painting on the passenger seat.

He drove off quietly. He had no idea where to go. He didn't turn his van around. Instead he continued to drive down the road. Binghamton was out of sight.

He was struggling to see the road. He realized he hadn't switched on his lights. He switched them on.

A large shadow of a building loomed ahead, lying across the road. Mateusz could hear crying. He glanced into the rear-view mirror. Urska was behind his shoulder, crying.

Mateusz screamed. He twisted the steering wheel, losing control of the vehicle. He slammed on the brakes and the van spun a 180-degree turn. He jumped out of the van, and ran backwards stopping in the middle of the road, his eyes open like saucers.

He stood staring at the van, he didn't breathe; he was too shocked. The rear door fell open.

Urska clambered out.

"Urska!" Mateusz shook his head.

"Mateusz," said Urska, disoriented.

Mateusz froze. She took a step forward, Mateusz instantly replied with the same step backwards. "You were dead?"

"Dead? no, the truck didn't hit me"

"But, but I felt your pulse?" Mateusz began to open his eyes wide in hope.
Urska, just began to shake her head and cry. "I don't know, I don't know, I must have been knocked out when I hit the floor"
"Oh my God, Oh my God" Bleeted Mateusz, he didn't breathe, he didn't dare, he was suspended, he was afraid anymove could burst this bubble, maybe it's a dream.

Urska dropped to her knees and sobbed

Mateusz ran to her, almost knocking her over with his embrace.

"Urska, I thought you were dead?" Mateusz burst into tears.

He ran his hands through her hair and pulled her to his torso.

"My darling," said Urska softly.

"I thought you were dead," cried Mateusz again.

Urska squeezed him tightly.

"Urska, Urska," he said.

The screams that Mateusz had released earlier into the woods were now met and defeated by screams of ultimate joy, an unbeatable joy that can be created only from the deliverance from such a tragedy, nothing less than a miracle.

They remained in this embrace. To do anything elkse but to remain in this embrace seemed pointless, now nothing else mattered.

Urska grabbed Mateusz's temples "We must see Stoneham."

"I have already seen him," said Mateusz as they broke ever

so siltly from their embrace.

"You have?" said Urska, her face buried back into Mateusz's

chest as she continued to squeeze him.

"Yes, he went into the painting." Said Mateusz.

"Into the painting?" Inquired Urska in a muffled tone.

"Yes, to save George, the Leyden boy."

"Oh my God. George is gone?"

"No, he *was* gone, Stoneham somehow got him back, but Stoneham is gone. I am going to burn it, destroy it," said Mateusz.

"No!" screamed Urska as she squeezed him even more tightly. "If you burn it, I am doomed."

She continued to squeeze. "You mustn't burn it."

"Please, Urska, don't squeeze so tight."

"You mustn't burn it," said Urska in a crackling voice two octaves lower.

If this was Urska in his arms, then who was it he could see, lying in the back of the van? Wasn't Urska dead? Yes, of course she was dead, he knew that, but his love had ignored logic, so now he held an imposter and this imposter held him. An imposter that began to laugh. A coarse, ugly laugh that came from a dead and rotting diaphragm.

The face that had been nestled into Mateusz's torso now eagerly began to reveal itself. This prospect surged into Mateusz's adrenaline system, allowing him to thrust away this deceitful demon.

He ran to the van without looking back at whatever it was, as the soulless imposter continued to laugh.

He opened the passenger door and grabbed the painting. He glanced at Urska, still at rest, untouched by the evil that surrounded him. The laughter stopped. Unsure where the ghoul had gone, he walked away from the van, and then began to circle it. Whatever it was, it was gone. Well, it wasn't there; he doubted it had really gone. He made his way back to his van with the same dread a bomb disposal expert feels on approaching suspect vehicles. He snatched some matches from the glove box quickly and nervously, like a macaque monkey snatching treats from a tourist; wary, untrusting.

He made his way tentatively to the back of the van. Next to Urska was a red plastic jerry can. He leaned into the van and grabbed it and shook it to see how full it was. There was enough gasoline. He leaned into the van and unravelled the blanket from Urska's face. He kissed her forehead. It began to rain, the cold drops hitting his back.

He looked around for somewhere to shelter, and to commit his act of valour.

With his destruction kit and the painting, he ran into the source of the large shadow that had engulfed the road, an abandoned mill.

The building was made from the same brick as Binghamton and easily as old. Where Binghamton had had a lobotomy, this building had been dissected post-mortem, remaining only a skeleton with some clumps of flesh. He stood and looked up at the four floors. All easily visible from the outside through the missing walls. He walked around the perimeter to find a way in. He came across a large metal door, which he worked open. Inside was a huge cast-iron square spiral staircase leading all the way up to the top floor, which was covered by a large tin roof. Huge gaps letting the raindrops that glistened on their way down to meet Mateusz's flickering eyes.

He ran up the stairs. Each floor was rendered useless in absence of a ceiling. But the top floor, that was OK, he could see it had enough of its ceiling to be of service.

It was a bar. *Was*, past tense, probably an executive room, once upon a time. Now upon this time, it was beyond rescue, even the fading laughter had actually faded. Now it was just rotten, the beer pumps rusted, one seized in mid-pump.

Mateusz walked behind the bar and placed the painting against a wooden shelf holding brittle bottles covered in dust.

He stood back and unscrewed the cap off the jerry can. He poured it over the painting.

The moment he did so, the very second, the screams of the boy engulfed the cavernous building. Mateusz spun around but there was nothing. The screams pervaded the very air, and when Mateusz inhaled, he felt he was breathing in these screams. He turned back to the painting, lit a match and held it to the canvas. The flame flickered out. Mateusz again looked behind him to locate the two demonic creatures. Still not there, but the screaming held his wits captive.

His hands trembling, he struggled to light the next match. He turned back to the painting, and now to his left stood the boy and the doll. The boy was screaming and holding out his arms to Mateusz. Mateusz shook his head. "Get away!" he screamed.

The boy and the doll began to walk toward Mateusz. This time, adrenaline was proving his enemy. His coordination was gone, and he dropped the match. He leaned back on the bar as he tried to pick up it up, rocking the rotten bar as he did so. The painting wobbled.

The boy's screams were deafening. The boy and the doll leaned toward Mateusz, who crumpled to the floor on his elbows. He was frantically striking matches one after the other, the light shining in from the gaps in the roof now revealing the demons' features clearly. The boy reached out. Mateusz fumbled to light another match, the last match. The boy's face began to change; his eyes began to sink as his face hollowed. Mateusz's own face began to whiten, thin blue veins appeared on his skin and his eyes too began to sink. He managed to light the last match in his trembling hands. He stood up and placed it to a corner of the painting, but it didn't light. Instead, Mateusz and the bar were engulfed in flames.

He buckled, knocking over the painting, which fell off the bar through a large opening in the floorboards. It travelled through the building, bouncing off objects as it fell through the broken floors.

Mateusz screamed in agony as the flames enveloped his body. He ran through the darkness out into the stairwell and stumbled toward the rusted railing, which collapsed, sending him to his death four floors below.

The Morning After

Captain O'Hara and an FBI agent stood looking up through the stairway standing next to the taped outline of where Mateusz's body had been found.

McCabe was speaking to the fire chief.

"So last night, you say?" said McCabe.

The fire chief sniffed the air and tapped his nose. "Yep." He looked around. "The body was a cinder, but wet. It was raining hard, the fire started up there." He indicated the top floor.

"We didn't come here because of the fire, there was some mess at Binghamton, an inmate escaped, and another one of the party, a witness, also left the scene. So the local PD found the van out there this morning and went inside here and found the body."

"So who was it? The escaped inmate?" asked McCabe.

"No," responded the fire chief. He held out a partially melted driver's license. "A Mateusz Boruch, unconfirmed though. There's a dead body in his van."

"Yeah, I heard about that," said McCabe "It all happens in the 'burbs, huh?"

O'Hara stood looking up at the burnt floor, turning around like a human antenna until he found a signal on his cell. He casually walked away from his new FBI companion.

"I think he burned the damn painting!" said O'Hara into his phone.

Gomez tried to find a private space away from Detective Vaden's ear. He made his way to a coffee machine and picked out a coffee through a succession of button presses.

"Why do you say that?" asked Gomez as he glanced over at Detective Vaden.

"Because it's not here, and the bar is burned to a stump, it stinks of gasoline and there's a melted jerry can, so he must have burned it. Damn it! Now we'll never know who the hell was behind this," said O'Hara. He continued, growing angrier. "Once you're done there with Vaden, I want a full report. It's a mess, Stoneham's escaped, Boruch dead, Leyden's lost his mind spouting all kinds of crazy things, this Urska chick dead, and now the Feds, wow the Feds, I have one with me, I have to go with him from here to their buildings for a status meeting. A full report, do you understand?"

"Yes, sir!" said Gomez. He gladly hung up the phone before O'Hara started an interrogation. *Burned*, he thought. He leaned back against the coffee machine and closed his eyes in relief. "Well done," he whispered.

"Something you wanna tell me, Detective Gomez?" said Detective Vaden.

Nine Months Later

The hydraulic arm of the excavator stretched up to the second floor. The operator peered through his reinforced cab screen and he tugged on a filter-less and bent cigarette. His excavator pulled away at the final remaining flesh of the mill. Huge chunks tumbled through the air.

He noticed something falling that wasn't brick or metal.

He switched off the engine and climbed out onto the right of the vehicle. He took another puff of his crooked cigarette and then rolled it off his lip and threw it behind his shoulder like spilled salt.

His lumbering frame made its way over to the object. He hobbled over broken girders and rocks like a fat tightrope walker. He bent down to pick it up. A curious co-worker, the only other person on site, dropped his pick-axe and joined him.

"Jesus, what the hell is that?" said the co-worker.

"It was on the second floor," said the driver in a heavy New York accent. "Creepy bastards, huh, …..creepy creepy bastards?"

"What are you gonna do with it?

The driver shrugged. "I dunno." He held it to the light. "Keep it, maybe."

The co-worker put his hand on the driver's back. "Keep it?"

"Why not?" insisted the driver.

"Why not? You said why yourself: 'Creepy bastards'."

"Then I'll sell it," said the driver.

"Who'd buy that?" quizzed the co-worker.

"You never know. It must be worth a buck. I'll put it on eBay."

"Holy shit," laughed the co-worker. "Be careful what you bid for."

The End

Made in the USA
Columbia, SC
26 November 2021

49779582R00217